BEYOND
SACRIFICE

BEYOND
SACRIFICE

Alicia Dill

CIRCUIT BREAKER BOOKS

Circuit Breaker Books LLC
Portland, OR
www.circuitbreakerbooks.com

Cover and book design by Vinnie Kinsella.

ISBN: 978-1-953639-08-0
eISBN: 978-1-953639-09-7
LCCN: 2021908388

This book is dedicated to those in harm's way.
Your service and sacrifice are a solid foundation to build a
life on. Remember to live it!

Chapter One

LA ARENA, AASIFA, AREIA, SABBIA, SAND. NO MATTER HOW MANY ways I cursed the word under my breath, it remained. In my hair, under my nails, in my shoes and all the fleshy cracks, there it was. Proof of time passing by, yet connecting me to a part of myself, precious and constant.

When I was little, I bottled it up everywhere I went with my parents, to the beaches in Miami, Argentina, Sardinia and New Zealand. Name the place and I had a bottle of its sand. I couldn't remember everything about those trips, but I saved the sand. My parents allowed me the particles of the beach, and that was no small thing for our family. My mom didn't want me to keep anything, no T-shirts, no souvenirs, nothing. She was a smart woman who didn't want to leave with evidence. Now she had a six-year-old with a box full of everywhere we'd been in the past few years. It was my dad who finally convinced her to let me keep up my collection.

"She spent so much time collecting it, why not let her keep it, mi amor?" he implored. With her nod of approval, my chubby hands eagerly dug large holes and shoved the wet clumps into plastic Fanta bottles, only to be forgotten as soon as we returned home and I abandoned them next to the igneous rocks from my Boricua grandfather.

What I could not know as a young collector was how arduous the journey would become. The sinking, sad feeling when no one would advocate for me, ever again. I was alone in a desert of the mind watching the tide roll in, nostalgic and dazed. The sand was the only real thing I could recognize.

As a freshly minted assassin, I understood the risks my mother had to take to give me any sort of a normal childhood, even in our short time together. I learned later that my parents were not active field agents with the CIA during those years, but old habits die hard. Information alone was dangerous to them, and I was still learning the reasons why. Now, I realized at twenty-eight years old, I was still living a life they kept choosing over me.

I shifted on my beach towel and tried to ignore the sand-throwing toddler to my right.

I turned my head, picturing the German mother removing the sand from her son's hands and taking him farther down the beach to play, but after the fifth ball hit my leg, I was done.

In my best Portuguese slang, I yelled for the man selling towels along the beach to come show me his collection.

"Hey man, I'll give you fifty dollars to get that lady and her son to move," I said, without removing my sunglasses. I wasn't even sure I had that much cash on me, but we would work something out.

"Nooooo problem," he said, his smile gleaming with gold. "Show me the money first."

"I have something in my purse besides cash," I said, making a local gesture for a gun.

Like a knight in shining armor, he begged the woman to buy a towel for a good three minutes before she picked up her stuff and ran away from the towel salesman. Not a moment too soon.

"My money, please?" he said, no longer deterred by my gun threat. He was back with several of his colleagues.

"Here's one hundred dollars," I said, as I gave him the only cash I had on me and took off my sunglasses. I wanted him to see my eyes. "No disturbances, understood?"

"Of course, we are like your personal bodyguards, whatever you need," one of the other men answered.

"Just let me enjoy the beach in peace. It's my only day off," I said as I lay back on the towel.

It was funny, because the guidebook warned this stretch of shore near the Copacabana was one of the most dangerous beaches in the world, a stark comparison to its beauty. But I didn't agree. All I encountered were perfect gentlemen, businessmen who understood money and power. If I wielded both correctly, I could kill them as fast as they would surely kill me, but we were both armed, unlike the blonde Frau and her child. If they killed me, no one would mourn my death. I was buried in the minds of my loved ones.

My identity as Concepcion Chapa was dead. Here I was, someone shiny and new with a carefully crafted identity, though unwilling and contemptuous of my circumstances. Was that even my real family? Were they my real parents? After a few blows to the head in training, I wasn't sure about anything that wasn't right in front of me. The good ole' existential crisis courtesy of the United States government, standard-issue and fully rejecting my understanding of what was and what could be. The term YODO, "you only die once," simply was not true.

After my untimely death, I knew my friends and relatives had moved on quickly, back to the lives they told themselves were important. All my friends, that is, except for Joelle. Joelle was more than a friend in the traditional sense. She was my battle buddy. In the Army's infinite genius, it paired us into teams of two. We were responsible for each other and endured every moment of embracing the suck together. It was all about accountability to a perfect stranger and reducing the misconduct that was common when breaking a person down to her core. "If it came down to it, you know I would die for you," I whispered to her from the top bunk of our barracks in basic training. The revelation scared me as soon as I said it.

"Yeah, but would you kill for me?" she said, laughing. Yeah. I would. I did. That was the point of all this. An average person couldn't expect that type of loyalty from anyone but soldiers.

This buddy system wasn't in all branches and all years but, once it was introduced post-9/11, it stuck. It worked, too, because my closest confidante still cared about her other half.

Joelle would take some time to move on from my death, but that was the genius of what brought us together. I hoped the death benefit I left to her through my lawyer, $400,000, would ease her pain. This was something the CIA grumbled about paying when faking my death, but since when did the government have a say in how I spent my cash? It was a cost benefit-analysis, and they wanted it to look real.

The whole saga started in 2008, the same time the financial crisis was ruining countless other lives. Not quite a year ago, after a long, uneventful day at the office examining crimes of the rich and guilty, the course of my life changed, such that I could never find my way back. I dropped my keys in the leaf by my condo door and took off one shoe before I smelled the scent of someone in the air.

"Chuey?" I said into the living room. "Is that you?"

I took off the other shoe and grabbed my keys. I was hoping it was Chuey Valderron, my fellow agent and live-in fiancé.

"No, it's not, Concepcion. It's me," a man's voice greeted me in the foyer.

"Sir, is that you?"

"It is."

I let my shoulders drop and walked into my small living room, decorated with the latest gray and lavender swatches, chosen to set my brain at ease. Why was he here like this? Something was wrong if my captain broke into my apartment. But he was family.

Captain David Aquila was seated on my loveseat with one ankle crossed at his knee. It looked as if he was stretching with a full blue Armani suit on. Beyond being my leader, Aquila worked with my late parents and ended up guiding my career once I was of the age to serve my country. A mentor and a surrogate uncle of sorts. "Where's Chuey? Que bolá?"

"He's still working on a case. Gianni and Chuey are getting it tonight," he said, his voice strained with something new.

I nodded. My fiancé and my fellow colleague at the Miami FBI office were making some real headway on a few cases that took more brains than brawn. I didn't have the patience for the lengthy investigations into data trails and forensic detection. I was a field officer. I needed to be out in the world.

"You want a cafecito, or something else? I'm so done after working today. We had that pedophile guy in for six hours before he gave us the names. I just can't..."

He shook his head no and gestured for me to feel free to caffeinate myself. I walked to the kitchen and started making a coffee with my cafetera. I packed in the granules and set the flame and turned around.

"I know you are wondering why I didn't set up a meeting. I will get to it. While I'm on the subject of you, you're doing estupenda. I'm really proud of what you've accomplished in the 305. You were gone too long playing soldier."

I hesitated. Silence was better right now. I was about to get fired. My skin flushed under my white button-up shirt. I hated wearing this starched basic. I didn't have a choice. It was suits and simple shirts for my profession. It made us more ambiguous.

"But there is something I need you to know and it is muy seria. That's why I came here." He shifted his weight and pulled a folder from inside his jacket. What an odd place to put it. His chest was at least an XL, a strong body for a sixty-plus year old.

"I'm ready." I checked my cafetera and watched as the gurgle of the coffee started to force the liquid up into the chamber. I turned back to Aquila.

"Concepcion... I have evidence that your parents are still alive. I believe it is true not only because of what I have in this folder but for a part I played in their disappearance."

The coffee was all the way up. I focused on pouring it into the small cup I bought with Chuey on a vacation at the Dominican Republic. The white and black letters made me think of that moment. The sun was so strong and warm that it hid all the little things wrong with our relationship for the entire week.

I took a sip and looked in Aquila's eyes. He stared into me. I kept drinking, sure of one thing—I needed this coffee. I wasn't going to entertain the idea that my parents were alive. Not for one second. That pain was sealed and not tolerable.

He continued, "All those years ago, we were part of an operation that blended the FBI and CIA into a specific team used for high-profile targets. We were forced to merge resources towards the end of the Clinton presidency in order to capture and kill war criminals from the various genocide and drug campaigns."

Aquila paused and waited while I rinsed my cup, "Are you even listening, mijita?"

"I've heard every word. Don't mijita me. I'm still waiting to hear something worth hearing."

"Don't be a fucking brat, la pequena mocosa, Concepcion. This is serious. I'm talking about your flesh and blood."

I sat near him on the couch. My flesh and blood were dead, and he was toying with the only memories I had left.

"Go on, then. You came all this way."

A turbulence started to build as I held my tongue.

"Your parents were the best we had, and because of them getting on board, we secured $200 million in funding from those spineless politicians. Anyways, I'll keep this part short. I didn't know exactly where Clara and Carlos were, but every time we hit a big target I thought was impossible, I thought of them. If it wasn't them that pulled the trigger, it was the team they built from the ground up. Those two, they are really something..."

"Does this story have a point? I know what they were, and it doesn't change anything for me." I gestured to my condo. It was decorated with all the latest design trends, but devoid of the love I'd felt when I was with my mom and dad. I thought of my parents' hopes and their disappointment in me. I ruined so many of their plans for my future. The feelings would never go away.

"The point is, Concepcion, that your parents are missing and haven't checked in. We have a request from their team to extract you and bring you on board to help locate them."

I crossed my hands and looked into the part of the ceiling where it met the wall. What Aquila was saying made no sense to me. I could not for one minute think my parents left me for a life of pain and loss. It was not possible.

"What exactly are you asking me? Pero que esta diciendo? Se es verdad, you lied to me for fifteen years and if you are lying now then…" I trailed off as tears started to flow with no thoughts that they were coming.

I thought of her. Clara, my mother, brushing my hair back and cutting me tiny pieces of raw coconut to eat with my morning cereal, saying, "This will make it grow strong." She was a force of nature, before she died. When dad was away on business and she was operating solo, she studied hours into the night to get her master's degree while preparing a full-course meal for my grandparents and me. Proud and self-possessed, she ensured we made do with whatever teacher's assistant stipend she received.

My father, Carlos, was always bursting with light energy, even after a long week of setting up high-end home alarm systems across the country, all from the back of an old, VW bus. He showed me how to do pull ups on the bar that hung in our kitchen, placed there only to impress Mom while she ignored his attempts for attention.

"Even if you can just do one, mija, you'll beat all the girls in your class," he said.

Aquila started again, but the memories brought a flush to my cheeks.

"This group has a higher authority than FBI and CIA, since those are managed in the public eye. If this team wants you, they get you. Specifically, because your parents have tracked your life the entire time. The team is nervous that your life is at risk if your parents were taken. Any photos, any technology linked back to you means the wrong people may use you against them. It's our idea to activate you, a proven asset, a killer who can be most useful in a different line of work."

"Who do you think you are, Aquila? Telling me it's already decided, and my only choice is putting my fate in your hands again? And for how long? What kind of life is that? What will Chuey say? My parents would never leave me. Not for one day, and if they did, then I don't care what happens to them. I can't."

Being an orphan was one thing, but abandoned as a teenager was something totally different. It was a choice.

"You don't mean that, Concepcion. You can't." He leaned back and patted the folder next to him. He acted so sure of himself. Latin men disgusted me with their machismo.

I wasn't taking the bait. He was going to show me some bullshit computer photos of my parents with wrinkles and different hair.

"I actually don't have time to argue with you." He stood up and looked down while I sat on the couch. "We are already starting to build the story of your disappearance. This mission is critical, and I can't let you risk your parents' lives over some hurt feelings."

"I have a choice, Aquila. I don't have to do whatever you say. I know enough to know the U.S. government doesn't blackmail its assets."

"Well, then you know nothing. Check the folder once I'm gone but know that we're picking you up tomorrow at the office. You can't tell Chuey or Gianni or your Army girlfriend, Joelle. No one! You are done being this spoiled brat. You're going to thank me someday when you're hugging them again."

I looked at my knees and waited for Aquila to leave. I heard the click of the door and then searched for my phone in my purse. A message from Chuey. It was still on silent mode from the ride home.

I'll be home late. Captain Crunch has us working the shit jobs. Gianni's drinking that mate' stuff that smells. Love you.

I smiled. His nickname for Aquila was an inside joke but the captain remained oblivious. It all stemmed from a Halloween photo on his desk with a pirate costume and an eye-patch. I convinced Gianni to drink mate' and after several failed efforts, he was now hooked to it.

Besides coffee, it was the only thing that pulled me through. The clock read 6:47 p.m. which meant I was losing daylight if I wanted to get a run in.

My inner debater was tempting me to open the glossy folder. If I opened it, I may not want to go on my run. Or maybe I should open it and the run would help me clear my thoughts about what was inside. I decided to do both and got ready with my running gear. Once I was completely Lycra-ed up, I sat on the couch. It was now or never.

Chapter Two

I OPENED THE FOLDER, WHICH WAS LIGHT. ONLY A FEW SHEETS of papers inside. Both were enough to convince me I was at the mercy of Captain Crunch Aquila, and my future was not my own.

"Oh, fuck!"

The first paper inside was a blown-up photograph, a still image from a video confession I made with two FBI agents while I was deployed in Iraq. My uniform was covered in the blood of another soldier, a bad seed that I rooted out with zero remorse. By confessing to these agents, I had received amnesty. They helped cover it up completely.

The person I killed was the son of a well-known senator from Louisiana. My crime should have been court marshaled, but my two agents were intelligent enough to know that if it got out—whatever had happened—it would look worse for the government. They could cover up my crime and be glad that I had ended Staff Sergeant Noel Evans' reign of terror. Evans's crime was personal to me. He raped one of the kitchen staff, a local Iraqi girl who came to work with her father. Prior to the act, she reminded me of a more delicate version of my young self. She confided in me after I came in from a tough mission outside the wire. She wasn't sure exactly what sex was and needed to know if she was going to become "instantly pregnant."

It wasn't his first offense or his last. For his various crimes, Evans was simply moved , thanks to the influence of his father.

A website he created at West Point was still trading nude photos of female soldiers to this day, despite many attempts to delete it. The damage was done. Some of those photos were from hidden cameras in basic training showers. And even more images were of civilian women spread eagle for their deployed boyfriends. Two of those photos were of my battle buddy and me dressing after a shower at the camp.

As a victim of sexual assault, I swallowed my tongue every time I thought of it. I would never say I was innocent of his killing. I carefully crafted what I was going to do as soon as I looked into the eyes of the girl. Her innocence was shattered like mine so many years ago. I was abused by my aunt's husband at fourteen years old and had an abortion. An experience too difficult to bear, too visceral to remember. By that time my mother, Clara, had started working more and more. Her hard-won career as a sociology professor took her and my father on long research sabbaticals, and I spent more time away from her watchful eyes. I thought she was giving me what I wanted, space, everyone to leave me the fuck alone. Like any teenager, I had my stuff. But at fifteen years old, I was an orphan. I couldn't tell her I wasn't a puta. That I was her good little mija, through and through. She was supposed to know I didn't consent. But it didn't matter now. The darkness found me. And it didn't let up. I had to build the fire that would keep me from ever being a victim again.

I waited until Evans was back from a mission. He liked to work out in the late hours, at 11 p.m. or even later. I couldn't risk any of the hundreds of cameras around the camp catching me. I wrapped a long burka around me, loosely, as I had had done jokingly with Joelle using our shower towels. She thought it made me look like Mother Mary from a cheap Bible movie. Little did she know I was practicing. I walked slowly as he was exiting the gym.

Jackpot! A predator like him couldn't resist finding out who was walking at almost midnight near an un-surveilled area of the camp. He jogged to me and wrapped his arm around my chest. He felt my uniform.

"What the fuck?"

I dropped my shoulders and let the fabric fall around me. I wanted him to know who he just grabbed.

I went straight for his throat with my Gerber knife. Twenty-one different ways I could use it. I stabbed three times on his carotid artery. He clutched at his throat and his eyes searched mine for a reason.

I hissed, "You can die not knowing, motherfucker. You've done enough and not even daddy can save you now."

As Evans dropped to his knees and bled out, I grabbed my disguise, using it to wipe my face off. Still sticky and full of adrenaline, I walked straight to the FBI compound. I knocked on their plastic Conex door and told them everything. Within twenty minutes, they moved the body outside the camp and made it look like he had wandered outside the wire and an unknown assailant took his life.

His senator father was able to mourn his son as a hero "to this great nation." All the while, fellow versions of Evans traded naked photographs of the women in uniform whose service somehow didn't measure up in the eyes of many Americans. Investigators blamed the Iraqi police force who worked alongside the U.S. forces. The girl he raped didn't talk to me anymore, but I could see in her eyes that she was changed by his death, and she was avenged.

It wasn't easy after that. I didn't get off Scot-free. The two agents kept the question and answer sessions up informally when I just wanted to put the killing in my past. Together, they decided they would shield me, though I never understood why. I was prepared for the punishment. I confessed to planning and executing the act, premediated murder. I took several psychological tests at their insistence, each one more and more in-depth, reminding me of my mother's chosen field of study. I wasn't sure why they needed to prove that I had it in me. When I told them what I practiced and whispered to Sgt. Evans, they were sure I was lying and covering for someone else.

"People I know are too freaked out to say anything..." the agent said, "let alone words from an action movie."

This comment only further enraged me, and I dug in. I said it, and I don't say things I don't mean.

"Why are you protecting me?" I asked. "This is going to get out."

Both told me to be grateful and shut my mouth. "Bigger things are at play than your bullshit vengeance."

I had showered in their private shower. I remembered using Axe body wash to scrub off the blood and left wearing sweatpants and a white tank top that said *vice* on it. When I came back to the room I shared with my roommate, Joelle turned on the lamp. She did a double take at my outfit.

"I'm not even going to ask where your uniform is," she said. "But looks like you had a grrreat time." I managed a smile. She was a picture of innocence to me. I wanted to kill the guy again for taking advantage of our private space and capturing us and thousands of other women in a vulnerable way. Never again.

I came back to myself. I was shaking holding the photo. It didn't faze me at the time that my confession was videotaped, but now it meant everything.

I shifted in my running pants and took out the second item in the folder. It was an affidavit from the two agents who reported covering up the murder and doing so as part of an agreement related to the War on Terror. What kind of reason was that? The agreement was signed by a state department official with a member of the CIA weighing in. What the hell was this?

The details of the event were clearly articulated. *The asset, Concepcion Chapa, will exit the Army post deployment and be managed in the future by Aquila.* Why was my life scripted here on the page?

I thought back to when I decided to join the FBI. It had sounded appealing. I got a $40,000 signing bonus and I was sure the Army was going to deploy me again in the stop-loss program. A perfect storm for me to pull my parachute out before the orders came down. I was obligated to do some good for an agency that shielded me despite its proclaimed values, Fidelity, Bravery and Integrity.

I pulled out the last page. It was an image of two good-look-ing, middle-aged people. Clara and Carlos. The woman was shorter and curvy, and the guy looked like he worked out. No handlebar mustache that used to bristle on my forehead when my dad would lean in for a kiss. This guy was clean-shaven. Not my parents. The nose was different for both and possibly the chin on the woman. She was laughing while seated in a street café, and he turned around in his chair next to her as if he was looking behind him.

"That's not them, but nice try, Aquila..." I whispered to myself.

I was wrong on so many levels. Concepcion Chapa was supposed to have died in a tragic car accident. The folder Aquila handed me before I left for a sort of training read Sofia Paltrini. I was officially separated from everything I once believed about myself. My body was supposedly disintegrated and sitting in a colorful urn in the Miami home of my adopted parents. At least, I hoped it was vibrant, tropic green and orange, please.

The one part of me that the U.S. government wanted to keep alive was the part that could kill on command. I was starting to get used to the cold sweats that kept me up at night. I liked being undead, like a vampire. Only instead of speed and super strength, I had bruises in all the wrong places, and I was very tired of being my new self.

These past few months were all part of the package my handler in the CIA called "additional training." I knew all about their *training*. They could cut off my nose and raise my cheekbones and call it training.

What I would never be trained for was how to be a normal, inconspicuous Argentinean woman on a beach in Brazil. The "farm," a secret training facility located somewhere in Virginia, was where they started my transformation. Even after discovering how to withstand torture, commit suicide, and, most importantly, how to drive a speed boat, I had so much more to learn. A longer stop at the Sherman Kent School for Intelligence Analysis gave me the tools to keep me safe during the intellectual battle of assuming a new identity. But the killing part, that was raw talent. That was what they hired me for and that was where the official paperwork stopped.

I was tired of thinking about the hell I just went through to get me mission-ready. Would my new identity ever be complete? I put my headphones in and lay on my back. I started my playlist of Bruce Springsteen songs.

The noise around me suddenly sounded far away, but the Jersey native Bruce Springsteen singing always gave me back something I left behind. My Americanness. Wow, everything revolved around me, pulling out the traces of my own upbringing. He was singing in my language and I listened as he sang, "That would take my God-filled soul and fill it with devils and dust." I wasn't emotional about home. More for the idea of it. Joelle and I loved "The Boss." Our years together involved too much introspection around Springsteen's lyrics. She was always my link back to the best part of me.

Joelle McCoy was my alter ego, my best friend, the one who didn't have the ingrained pain of loss. She was what we all hoped we could be if the world worked the way it did in a novel. Her emotions were all over her face, and I needed that. I allowed myself her friendship, and I hid the worst parts of myself to shield her from knowing. This helped me now that I couldn't see her, ever again.

I met Joelle in basic training. The Army chose her for me but ultimately we made our friendship our own. We were accountable to each other in those nine weeks but that tie was never broken, until now. I thought it was enough to be a female soldier, a lone wolf, but wherever we went, we chose to be together. The catty backbiting that comes with close quarters never took hold. I clawed the sand in front of me, digging a hole with my manicured hand.

She understood my feelings about my parents better than anyone else in the military.

"You can't think of it that way, Chapa," she said, arranging my dark hair into a sock bun as we prepared for our going away ceremony at a high school. "Not everyone has someone here to see them off. It's not really a big deal, anyways."

We were both dressed in our Army Combat Uniforms, fresh with thickly-applied matte makeup hiding our tired eyes, but we couldn't help our aching backs. Joelle tried to cheer me up and explain that a deployment ceremony was just a dog and pony show. Not a big deal to someone who has eight people here for her.

I smiled for Joelle's family as her mom cried again and again, tears streaking her mascara. I stood next to my best friend and watched her dad walk away in sadness. It was too much. It was everything I wished I had. My memories of my childhood were still raw. I held onto the few things I could remember about Clara and Carlos, my real parents. Snippets of busy career people with our small family at the center of it. My mother a professor, an intellectual who planned our life down to the last detail. Her voice was the architect I missed when I had to face a tough decision, though she raised me well enough to think for myself and be independent even when I longed for the safety of a group. I didn't share everything with Joelle. My mother taught me the art of withholding knowledge for our family's safety, and, most of all, to protect our feelings. If she caught a whiff of someone asking too many questions, she would shut down the conversations and turn the tables on whoever was curious about our life. It didn't matter if they were family or not.

She would never have displayed emotion at a graduation like Joelle's mom, let loose. And my mother knew exactly how to handle my father when his grand plans and storytelling overtook the room. The image of a handsome young couple who poured their free time into a rebellious, angsty teenager never left me at important events—nor did the memory of my own failure to be grateful for their care and attention. I missed the constancy of my parents, the analytical poise of one parent and the friendly coach in the other.

I longed for their approval and even forgiveness. This ceremony would have made them proud to witness my sacrifice, my service.

"Are you coming to eat with us, Chapa?" Joelle's sister, LaLa asked. "I can't deal with mom by myself and Joelle needs her battle buddy."

I nodded. Yes, I was going to dinner. What else was I going to do while everyone spent their last day with those who loved them. "Only if it's good," I said. "And I'm buying your mom a margarita. She's way more fun after a few of those."

"Fun for you maybe," Joelle said, patting her sister on the back. She was the one who brought us all together.

"Don't pat me!" LaLa said. "You know I hate that shit."

Joelle patted her butt and laughed. "You know, just because you said that, I'm going to pat you all night long."

They exchanged glares and then burst out laughing. Sisters.

I missed the sibling I would never have. As a young child I dared to ask my mother why I didn't have a sister or a brother. As she was driving around in our weathered Honda Accord, she turned back and said, "That could never happen."

I persisted, "Why not?"

"Well, honey," she said, hesitating, "it's not part of the plan." That was that. I didn't ask my dad because his usual response was to "ask your mother."

Joelle was the best version of her true self around her sisters. And that made her the best around me. Her feminine energy gave me permission to unravel, to laugh, to live. We were soldiers and no one else could understand. I shook her dad's hand when we finally got ready to get on the bus. He pulled me back in and hugged me close. His breath hot on my ears, "You bring her back safe, ya hear."

I reached up to his tall frame and kissed his cheek. "I promise I will."

As the bus rolled away and Joelle was peering out behind, her dad yelled through the opened window, "I'm countin' on you!"

She smiled back, but I knew he meant me. He was counting on me to take care of his girl. And now I wasn't ever going to be able to make that promise again.

I wiped away the tears and rolled onto my belly, coming back to myself. I removed my headphones and cried into my towel, laid out on the white sand. I wanted to make sure I didn't cry too loud and bring back my favorite towel salesman. My new, swollen nose pressed into the Hilton hotel towel. Its new form caused the most excruciating pain. What was I doing crying on the beach? This was my only scheduled pity party for days and I had to make the most of it. And with a bottle of wine awaiting me in the small cooler, I would get all the crying out. Was I mourning the loss of myself? Or was I just feeling alone in my new world? This bottle was for me, the end of my short life. The next song on my new life's playlist: "Working On a Dream."

Just as I was polishing off my second glass of Pinot Noir, I heard the low vibration of my cell phone. It was my handler, Charles Huntington, my only link to my new life—a life that was supposed to lead me to my family.

"Hello, my dearest darling," Charles Huntington said, in his best impression of British royalty. "How is the beach?"

"It's beautiful this time of year," I said. "Everyone is so much friendlier around here."

"Love, tell me you didn't make any new enemies during your free time," he said. "I don't want to think about anything happening to you."

"No enemies, more like friends. And I did catch something. It was the sweet smell of freedom," I answered, smiling at the thought of him here at this beach with me.

"Oh, you Americans and your freedom, couldn't you just have paid the taxes on the damn tea," he said. "We paid them, and we turned out fine."

"You sure did, that's why you're working for us," I said, changing the subject. "By the way I'm going to need a ride back to the hotel. Some of these new friends might want to see what else is in my new Gucci bag."

A long sigh.

"Why couldn't you have just stayed at the hotel? They have an infinity pool with controlled temperature and more importantly security," he said.

"Too many tourists. It's my only day off and I wanted to hang out with the real cariocas," I said. "You people don't know how to have a good time. I want to feel the heart of the people, and where else but the beach?"

"Fine...I already sent someone," Charles said.

"Is he cute?"

"You'll just have to find out."

"Oh, boy," I said, as I walked off the beach, hot sand filling my shoes with every step. "I love when you surprise me."

The bellboy of the plush hotel took one look at my new face and straightened his jacket.

"Can I help you, miss?" he said in fluent Portuguese.

He shifted his weight as he carried my heavy suitcases, full of designer clothes, mostly shoes. The gun was the most important thing, and I had it on me. The least expensive item in comparison to my five-inch stilettos. My new camouflage was style and excess. On some level, it was a protection and a risk. It afforded me anonymity, as wealthy people are accustomed to privacy. Dressing in my camouflage or even an all-black uniform would have set all the tongues wagging.

Once I settled into my hotel room, I changed into my other outfit, a tailored but forgettable Calvin Klein suit and Prada black leather shoes.

I put a bar glass up to the wall. The shower was running, and the television was on. A naked man made everything so much easier. My lucky day.

I checked whether the lock was left open per the plan. I eased the door open to my adjoining room. The bathroom door was open with a pile of clothes on the bed. With one gloved finger, I quickly checked the ID in the man's worn leather wallet on the nightstand.

It was him, Mr. Unlucky tonight. I stalked to the bathroom and pulled back the curtain. A stunned elderly man instinctively put his hands up to his face. Sorry, that wasn't going to help.

I fired three rounds square into his chest. Two more for good measure. I knew the first one was enough.

I backed out of the bathroom and returned to my own room, locking the door behind me. I turned my television up; unfortunately, it was the hotel's announcement channel, which played the same Samba beat on rotation. Like two hundred million other people, I was in Brazil. I didn't need to hear the Hilton's prepackaged version of this country.

Now safe, I unscrewed the silencer, stripped off my clothes, and handed the bag of bloody clothes to the colleague now hovering over the balcony, a nameless man with a round face. This man was managed by Charles but I wasn't sure if he was full agent. His job was show up, lift up, and shut up. Now in my underwear, stockings, and bra, I climbed into my hotel bed. I turned the TV on and flipped through the channels until I found a black and white movie. The channel was called Amor. My kind of channel. Sentimental much?

During a commercial break, I ordered room service to solidify my weepy mood. This hotel catered to foreigners and I was over acting like I had somewhere to be. Just a business trip. I slid further into the tightly made king-size bed.

No one knew I was here except for Charles and the backup guy. Well, this was how it should be. The onscreen couple started to lip-lock and I began to squirm. It was always the kissing that turned me on so much more than the sex. Sex was dirty and usually messy; kissing was the ultimate type of intimacy. Old movies were the perfect medicine, always with a happy ending.

My heart started to beat harder inside my chest, not Concepcion's chest, no, the new me complete with newly purchased body parts. Would this clean my conscience? Would this clean me up? No, the silicone was only another change that my new life demanded. Advantages and disguises, the stuff of espionage. This was the order of the day. I drifted off and slept soundly. Not like my old life. It must be a sign of better things to come. My reaction to this change in career was only that it was better than an Iraqi or Fort Leavenworth military prison stay for killing a fellow soldier.

It was ten thirty in the morning. The body was discovered minutes before. I had plenty of time to sleep late and eat a hearty breakfast at the café across the street. By the time the police arrived, the support team from Charles had taken over surveillance of the scene and I was free to take in the other parts of city. I looked up to see the Christo standing with his hands outstretched. I reached back to the figure of Christ. A strange thought. Did Charles assign me a religion under my new identity? For now, it was money and waiting for what started this farce.

Though I had already accrued well over a million dollars in my account, it still gave me a thrill to see a deposit of fifty thousand dollars for a single night's work. My job in the whole operation took the least amount of time. Someone else put in the long hours of planning and research. By the time I was assigned the case, all other means of limiting a threat had been exhausted and whomever it was I encountered was a walking dead man.

Two hours later, I was down about a thousand dollars from jewelry alone. I didn't even like what I bought. I would have preferred a souped up car, but that was too flashy for now. I hadn't considered the money I would earn, but it was part of the assignment that I look good spending it. This amount would be considered a fortune to any one of Rio's citizens living in the favelas. Maybe I could ask Charles to give a donation with parts of my fee; a few families could prosper with the blood money of someone else's death.

The more I acted like someone else, the more I became someone else. And just like Aquila explained to me, I was perfect for this kind of work. Gone were my origins as a righteous killer. It was don't ask, don't tell when it came to the targets of my profession. They had to be bad, right? Otherwise, why would the CIA want them killed? Thinking about those subjects would just make my life harder than it already was.

In one of my lower moments, I asked Aquila if he thought my parents would be happy that he was getting me into this team, the agency. He seemed so sure this was the only way to help his friends, but, on some level, he was betraying the life I wanted for myself. I missed my friends and I missed Chuey. We didn't have much except careers, but we had each other. In my previous assignment, I had a messy life that I mostly shared with the people I loved. My work was life. It was true that I had a dark side. I killed a man in cold blood without orders. I murdered him. And I hid it from everyone. But so what? Everyone had secrets.

Joelle didn't know me completely. She turned inward and I let her believe what she wanted to believe about me. I couldn't go to her anymore. But I still loved her. I still deserved a friend through all the shit.

With Chuey, my FBI life was comfortable with just enough excitement to make me a gray-haired trope of a Latina detective. I was happy and I had something that was mine. This was a mission to save something I lost years ago, my family. When was my choice?

Shopping for lingerie in an Italian designer store, I looked like I belonged here.

"Would you like to see these modeled?" an older, but styled woman asked as she pointed to a group of younger women. She spoke in Portuguese and I nodded. I minimized the amount of words I spoke in all the stores.

I was unsteady with my new accent. I needed to establish a plausible cover for how I spent my day. Who was I kidding? The police didn't even know I had killed last night or any night for that matter. The victim was a foreigner though, and I hoped they didn't try and truly investigate.

In a city of six million, I didn't see how they could. I was a ghost.

I bought everything the girls showed me and only one of the store models had a better hourglass shape than mine. Hers was natural so I had to give it to her. Mine was simply the best money could buy.

I managed to make some small talk towards the end, but the sales lady only smiled when she saw my black platinum MasterCard.

I glanced at my watch. It was three p.m. Surely things would die down at the hotel. It was the perfect time for a late lunch and a nap.

I woke up sweating, and, sadly, I was getting used to it. The hotel room felt chilly from the air conditioner working overtime, but the back of my neck was still damp with perspiration. What a dream. The images usually came to me only in the night, but it wasn't even six p.m. yet. I checked both of my cell phones; no calls, and no messages. Good sign. I stared up at the ceiling and closed my eyes again. I willed myself to think about something good, something comforting, but my own subconscious wouldn't allow it. I slept too well last night. These nightmares must be my gut-wrenching punishment. Damnation rolled off me in waves.

"This will pass, this will pass," I murmured. My torment had little to do with my present occupation; in fact, this kind of work gave me plenty of ways to escape.

I didn't have to face the world as Concepcion anymore, and it made all the lies I told myself a little more believable.

In my sleep, I dreamt about a pile of mutilated body parts on the side of the road. The sight of rotting human flesh still stuck in my mind. These parts were the bodies of two Arabic translators who were followed after working in our camp.

I hated the way the guys who shared that experience with me blamed the young women for their own deaths. Weren't we the same? The two translators and me? We were both trying to prove ourselves in a man's world. The Iraqis had a stake in our success, and I couldn't help feeling bad for their families. The women could have been killed by someone close to their families, but the local police had no leads. We had gone on the offensive six months prior, and, thanks to propaganda about driving out sectarian violence, a relative calm had recently settled over the village. Until the murder of two twenty-something, educated, pro-western women who were hacked into unrecognizable pieces.

"You identified with these women," a private shrink had said. "You have survivor's guilt. Why them instead of me?"

Seeing a mental health professional was a no-no. I saw the psychiatrist off the books. This ensured my psychological profile stayed clean for any government agency. I'm not sure where those tests from the FBI agents ended up after my confession. Aquila explained how important it was to hide any weaknesses while we were still employed, and that lesson stayed with me. Many of my psychiatrist's clients were former military. Secrets were not a problem. It was a very lucrative business.

I didn't share the story with anyone outside my chain of command, and, honestly, they didn't want to hear it. But those dead women from deployment woke me up at night more and more once I started working with the agency. My body count was now part of my daily life. I rarely thought about the men I killed. In one situation, two Yemeni men drove a dusty looking four-banger right up to the gate even after they were warned to stop. Everyone knew they had to be searched before approaching the gate, so it couldn't have been a worker. The other gate guard, Private First-Class Jamie Jackson, shot the driver, but it was me who killed the other man.

I still remembered those words Jackson said. "Concepcion took the last one out." The others seemed proud of me, except for Joelle, who just looked at me like I was the enemy. She would never understand what I was doing, then or now. I questioned what she would have thought about killing a fellow soldier.

"Was there evidence of an actual threat found in the vehicle?" she asked, voicing the question I didn't want to ask myself about the Yemeni drivers.

"We couldn't find anything, but we'll keep looking," I replied.

Believe me, we searched. My insides, where I was supposed to feel something, contained nothing for the man. Nothing for the life I ended. It was the uncertainty around who he was and why he was trying to get onto the base that made it okay.

The nightmares about the women translators were my cross to bear. Women were Madonnas to me, and so men had to be evil. Atonement wouldn't come easy. I stared up at the peach-colored ceiling of the hotel room and eventually fell back to sleep. Cognitive dissonance was my strength now; being human was my weakness.

I took the bondinho, an electric tramway, with the rest of the tourists.

"It is all part of the experience," Charles said, then passed me his handy weathered guidebook of all the quirkiest parts of the city. "Guard this book with your life."

I wanted some good dancing and male company. Too bad Charles didn't put male escorts in the book. I shouldn't have to pay for it, though. Quality free sex just might take a little longer.

The coldness of my exploits made me miss one other person from Concepcion's life. Though I could never fully commit everything to Chuey Valderron, he was mine. Unfortunately, he loved a woman who was unreliable and fractured in every way. I almost let myself go and marry him. Too good to be true. I sabotaged it before he could convince me to try. It was convenient, not only to die as Concepcion but also to avoid facing a breakup. This way Concepcion got off free and clear; she remained decent. And Paltrini was something else entirely.

Chapter Three

IN MY DARK MOMENTS, THE GRAVITY OF MY NEW IDENTITY weighed heavily on my soul. I didn't access the parts of me that were still "me" regularly, but they existed. During my CIA training, I'd learned to explore my old self, before the months of nothing but new. It didn't make me a complete person, but it would take a lifetime to do that. Reconciling parts of the old me and turning the page to a new beginning. It was a crawl, walk, run timeline of change. I would be crawling indefinitely.

Staring at a little green tree at the National Bonsai Museum during my time at CIA training gave me a sense of what I'm capable of. This tree was almost 400 years old and survived the Hiroshima bombing in World War II, tended by the same family, the Yamaki, before being gifted to the United States. I thought about the Yamaki family with five generations. This family had strong roots and delivered a precious gift, nurtured by time and tenderness. I had no such family, and my roots were hanging on by a few threads of contacts in the before and after. I thought about the trees I held close to my heart and the ones I would see in my future. And this tree was life. Everything was upended in its world and yet it remained. Just as I remained. It was replanted and that was the task before me, creating the me that fulfilled my mission.

Our instructor, a forty-something trainer, gave us an exercise about identity. We would discuss our findings as a group. All the head-shrinking assessments had left me bereft of what exactly I was supposed to do or say. I didn't want this post, so if they didn't like what I said, what was the outcome for me? Go back home? I was officially dead. I was unconvinced they would ever let me go. I would just be recycled into another job that put me in harm's way.

I sat at the plastic table in a gray furnished classroom and wrote the questions as the trainer gave us our instructions.

"Before you can go forward, you need to go back," she said. As she started to write the assignment on the white board, streaks of marker created a thin veil of its last gasps of ink.

"Why is cultural identity important? What is the identity you are leaving behind? What pieces of that identity can help you in your new one? How can you move past the grieving stage for your old identity to embrace the new you?"

I stared straight ahead as the rest of the class, three other recruits, started writing notes. My mind was blank. Nothing came to mind. A girl disrupted. My culture was this culture, service above self, a family to call my own. My parents and my adopted parents were part of a past that left me empty somehow. My military relationships, my FBI colleagues—those were my culture.

The instructor approached. "You need to write something, Concepcion," she said. "This is all part of the process. If you at least try to participate, I promise you, I can help you. Either way, you will sit here until our time is up."

Like many teachers before her, she was adept at dealing with me, an uneasy student. I wrote.

I started my list on my yellow legal pad. Who was I?

Concepcion Chapa, Army veteran, FBI Special Agent, Miami-raised, 305-for life! Daughter of CIA agents who died when I was

15 years old, with a Puerto Rican household. Family limited and not close. Girlfriend of Chuey Valderron, Dark curled hair, narrow eyes, flat nose, short, petite. My deceased grandparents came from Puerto Rico. I had some aunts and cousins living in Miami. But family was not like in the movies. We weren't close, passionate people living as one family unit with multiple generations, my parents careers were far too important for us to have that bond and live that life. My parents taught me to be strong, independent, and take risks that made sense. We were the only ones in my family who had an American flag that was bigger than our Puerto Rican one.

I stopped writing and remembered my father hanging the large American flag next to a smaller Puerto Rican one. My mother seemed upset by the difference in size as her family was very patriotic when it came to the old country.

"Arrogance gets you killed, Clara, and you should know that," he said. "We don't need to announce ourselves all the time."

The flags were an indicator of something beneath the surface that, even as a teenager, I couldn't put my finger on. The hours my mother spent with her nose in a book or training at the krav maga studio. Or the weeklong trips my parents needed to go on together while I stayed with family friends. The religious traditions we "didn't waste our time on," even as all my cousins went to confirmation. Still, despite dismissing the faith of my larger family, my mother always wore a small crucifix on her neck. The circles we drove in if anyone was following us too closely as we made our way home. Was this my culture, my upbringing? The fear and control that must have shadowed every decision my parents made after their long careers in the agency. Would this legacy serve me now?

ALICIA DILL

I wasn't quite finished, but the teacher interrupted my furious scribbling.

"Class, let's start with Concepcion. Kyle, tell me what you see with Concepcion," she said, pointing to the former Signals Intelligence Analyst with kind eyes. He was always smiling at me and saying, "It's going to be ok. No worries." I wondered how they roped him into this.

Kyle looked at her, "I see a female, a woman, youngish," he said.

"Is that it, Kyle?"

"I guess... Oh and she's a Latina, if that's the right term," he said, looking down. This guy wasn't sure about anything female. The CIA was going to eat him alive.

"Ok, great, Kyle," she said. "Now, Concepcion, how would you identify yourself."

I reviewed my written notes and decided against a long narrative.

"Well, he's right. I am a female and a woman," I said. "Latina is a correct term. I use the term, but I don't identify with it."

"Great, explain what you mean by that," she said. "You use the term Latina, but you don't identify with it? Haven't heard that before."

"It's a long answer," I said. "It's like saying, I'm an American born in the 305 of Miami. True, but it's very broad and doesn't really mean anything except geographic location. I'm proud of all the specifics. It's not the most important thing about me."

"So what do you identify with?" she asked. "This is important for us all to understand."

I looked around the room, two black guys and one white guy. An elite group of future assets.

34

"Identity? I'm an American, my parents and their parents were Americans, born in Puerto Rico which is...surprise! Part of the United States. A lot of people don't understand, so I usually have to correct them. But if I'm being honest, kind of the point here, who I am and where I come from changed when my parents died. I became an orphan and that was the part of my identity that most people brought up around me. Yes, I had adoptive parents, but then again, they were immigrants and refugees from war. We didn't understand each other most of the time. But they were kind and that was enough. I had a long-term boyfriend, also from Miami with mixed heritage, an American, and his Latin-ness wasn't what appealed to me. My real identity was my Army service. It was the first time I chose what I wanted to be. I wasn't born a soldier. I chose it. It was the only time in my life where I fit in."

"Correct me if I'm wrong, Concepcion," she said, biting on the end of her pen. She was a few bites away from tasting something. "You are not really identifying with the Latina culture because your upbringing was stunted by the death of your parents. And the Army culture was your family, your culture. The one you identify with now?"

Kyle nodded, understanding the instructor but glancing back at his paper.

"Yeah, I guess," I said. "But the word Latina is going to be different depending on the individual. My parents didn't make it a point to highlight our heritage as the most important part of who we were together. My point is that labels aren't really my thing, and we're here because we align with something bigger than the location we're from. That sacrifice is something my parents understood and passed down."

"Great point," she said. "Now, let's continue..."

And like that, my past was in the past and my future identity was created. Someone up high chose Argentina as my country of origin for my passport. My next assignment was understanding who I would become. I had no hope of ever truly passing as a native of Argentina with Argentinians, but the goal was to start with a clean slate that I could layer other experiences on to in order to complete my mission.

My immersion into Argentine culture brought me into contact with my case officer, who explained I was now an Argentinian of Italian descent, a global traveler, returning home to the country after years abroad, the basis for my identity.

"Right, but you have to think of these as different identities, so whatever parts you identify with from your Puerto Rican heritage, this is something totally different. Argentinians work to be seen as a mix of European, Italian, Spanish, German influences. The immigration is very similar to the United States," he said.

"Ok, so I get they don't reggaetón but flamenco instead, right?" I asked.

"The dances are different, but it's bigger than getting one thing right, one dance right. What do you want to take away from your Puerto Rican heritage? The island mentality, the pride, a stand-alone place that gives you an American passport. This can help you in Argentina as you assume the characteristics of someone else with an expressive, proud, passionate nature. "

"Why Argentina?" I asked him, as he was responsible for my transition.

"We have a lot of assets successfully relocated there. It's historically a perfect place for us as a jumping off point. And we just freed up a villa with your name on it."

A villa? That was why I had to pronounce yo and llamar like "sho" and "shamar." An impossible task, trying not to sound fake every two seconds. Leave it to the government to make real estate the direction my life takes. But accents were not the hardest part, though mine was still an attempt at a mix of Buenos Aires and posh Northern European Italian. I had no idea what was to come from the physical conversion side.

The surgeries took place in Colombia, where South American bellezza was just a few slices away.

"One of the most dangerous technologies for you, as the asset, is facial recognition technology. Your ability to roam the world undetected is close to zero because of this incredible leap in artificial intelligence. It's why we're going to break your nose and raise your forehead. And it may not be the only time in your life. This is the first step. Fillers can help keep the surgeries to a minimum so we don't have a Michael Jackson situation on our hands, but we have to stay anonymous and wigs and glasses aren't what they used to be," the male surgeon said.

My case officer continued, "Even with the surgeries, you are going to learn to use prosthetics. This is your life and the success of your mission. The world's best known assets are known in all government circles and criminal organizations that can afford the software. We are changing you to protect you, but that will come with a cost. You wouldn't be here if there were any other way."

And right before I wanted to jump off the nearest bridge to avoid the pain of transformation, I got the hard sell.

"We use surgeons who are particularly adept at the aesthetic we need for you. Lucky for you, Concepcion, South America is second only to South Korea in plastic surgery. We have the best of the best at our fingertips. And more importantly, many of your fellow Argentinians, not to mention Colombians or Brazilians, have gone under the knife. If someone sees how perfectly high and sculpted your nose is going to look, it won't matter if they can spot the work. It's part of maintenance for many girls your age, he said. "Trust me, it's an art."

I was still grieving the makeover and would be for a long time. I realized later my fellow students from the farm weren't leaving their real lives behind forever; they were just on temporary assignment. The crew chief and the other students left, hopeful and full of vigor to save the world. I wasn't going to be so lucky with my criminal history. This was permanent. These jobs were not listed in any sort of brochure. I had no idea how many people underwent a journey like mine, but with politically advantageous "accidents" happening all over the world, I was reminded that this was not a trial period.

Culture was not transferable, but I had to learn to adapt. Hot and cold, mind games, lots of socializing, dramatic, expressive, passionate, resent the labels, that was the key to my safety. Be Argentinian, feel in your bones who you are.

"Can I not do this?" I begged my case officer the night before surgery. My eyes swollen with tears.

He firmly shook his head no. "It was decided. You should have thought about that before you killed the son of a senator. Your confession was leaked. He knows. The old asshole was planning to off you himself. Killing the identity of Concepcion Chapa is the only win-win we are going to get out of this shit show."

I wiped my tears away and resigned myself to the new me. The die was cast and my fate was not in my hands. But at least I had been effective. I had shut down a predator. No more shame. And I still exist.

That night I dreamt of my mother. It was years since I saw her face so clearly. She was wrapped in her bath towel, smiling and putting her natural curly hair up with a velvet scrunchie. She was applying her makeup at her vanity mirror, singing Paula Abdul's "He's a cold-hearted snake, look into his eyes..." I was imitating her singing, with my hands on her shoulders. Wanting to be close to her. Her laugh. "Just like her mama."

She rarely showed humor outside of my nuclear family. The daughter of traditional parents, Clara rejected the feminine mystique. Yes, she did all the things that other women do. She married, she had a child, but she was a dedicated scholar, an educator, and she served her country during significant political shifts both in the United States and around the globe. The feverish question that remained after I woke up: why was I born? I wasn't sure my mother planned my birth. Her partner in every sense of the word was my father. It was obvious how much love and healthy debate passed between them. Watching their relationship, I was reminded of how my existence changed their dynamic. They loved me, but did they want me? My instincts told me the truth. But I couldn't focus on the past any longer, because the present was already scary enough.

Chapter Four

ACCEPTANCE WAS KEY IN GETTING ME THROUGH THE DAY. IT TOOK only two more months of work and I earned my first vacation. When all was said and done, I completed eleven contracts for the agency. All the while, the only word about my "parents" was that they were in deep cover in Asia, and that their fate was still in question. It was my responsibility to prove that I could go in once they were located for a possible rescue. It sounded like more bullshit to me, but I was a grunt who took orders.

"You need a break, mamasita," Charles said. "Too much too soon."

He assured me that I needed to take time out to enjoy the fruits of my labor, otherwise I'd burn out. Ironic, as I couldn't even visit the country I was supposed to be protecting. Freedom demanded a sacrifice, and my life was that tribute. But it was better to ask for forgiveness than permission, and, sanctioned or not, I wanted to go home.

As luck would have it, after completing a mission in the Bahamas, I found myself on a yacht headed back to my home-town, Miami. The older gentleman picked me up at a fancy hotel bar with a few too many laugh lines and insisted I see his gothic-style mansion in Coconut Grove up close.

I told him I'd never had the pleasure of seeing the city and he demanded we visit together, no customs check required.

A perfect way to travel as an Argentinian castaway—at least that's what he thought.

After he tried to seduce me, I contemplated all the ways I could let him down. When the man passed out from exhaustion closer to shore, I snuck into the harbor with only a few vital items and most of the cash he had under the bar. Back home with no identity, and no strings, flush with a few lines of cocaine from my yacht party, I was fully in vacation-mode in my old stomping grounds.

In a South Beach hotel, I dialed my ex-fiancé Chuey Valderron's number from memory just to hear his voice. Disgracefully, I did this without regard for privacy. I wanted the numbers to show up on his caller ID. I listened.

"Hello, hello, who is this?" my ex said. "Stop fucking calling here. I am tracking this number you little punk." Valderron repeated many of the same threats I'd heard before, but he was there.

I had used a satellite phone to reach out anonymously a few times while I was in Colombia, after my faked death. It was supposed to be a top-secret facility. But the staff left me on bed rest with a lot of painkillers and a phone at my bedside, still reeling from my life change. I dialed nine and then from memory I dialed everyone I was still missing.

No other women answered his cell phone, and that made me feel something like content. After Valderron, I dialed Joelle's home number in Missouri but got her voicemail. No, I wasn't going to leave a message no matter how nicely she asked. Being this close to everybody was harder than I thought. They wouldn't even recognize me if they stared right at me.

Perspiration dripped from my décolleté. Why was I sweating so much? The coke? Or the excitement of toying with my existence. Giggling, I kept up the crazy.

I called my adopted parents. Jimm and Chantrea's home number, my own once upon a time. Chantrea answered on the second ring. After a long pause, Chantrea whispered to Jimm that it was a telemarketer, and he told her to hang up. She asked once more, "Can you hear me?" And she muttered something. If any of them tracked the number, it would lead them right to my hotel and the possibility thrilled me. A little too much.

The reality of what I had done settled in as the euphoria dissipated.

"Charles," I said.

"Yes," he answered, annoyed at the unscheduled call.

"I fucked up. Code drunk." No need to mention any other substances.

I blamed it on the small bottles of alcohol from the mini fridge. Sitting on the floor drinking from the tiny bottles like Alice in Wonderland, I looked up to see a large bodyguard type enter my room. Without a word, he scooped me up in his arms. I didn't resist.

Fucking Charles. An hour later I was in another hotel. My first free days and he had to rescue me from this place. I was supposed to be in the Bahamas.

I missed my old life. It made no sense to me in the early morning hours of my third trip to the bathroom.

Sitting in the empty hotel bathtub with half my clothes on, I used the halogen lighting to examine my hands. My polished French tip nails masked the stubbiness of my fingers. These two hands could always identify me. The same small scar from bayonet training in boot camp remained between the fleshy part of my ring finger and thumb. It comforted me, and at the same filled my gut with ulcers.

How much worse could it get? Blackmailed into a life I didn't want. Being a contract killer, with no sense of duty or allegiance to my country. Married only to the idea that the people who raised me were still alive. What was the next step if I proved unstable? What was the Plan B for me? I wanted some Cubano food from the tienda near the old neighborhood. Pastelitos instead of empanadas. It wouldn't give me peace, but it would at least fill my stomach.

Still buzzed, I put on my slip of a dress and went downstairs. I watched from the elevator as the hotel staff set up the complimentary breakfast buffet. This was not what I considered hangover fare. Though I looked a little too much like a high-class escort finishing out a long night on the job, I made my way back to the front desk to get a ride to some good food.

"Perdona, where is ventanitas? Pastelitos?" I managed to say in my best-accented English. This lady might know the difference.

"There is one a few blocks down on the left. Would you like me to call you a taxi, ma'am?"

The middle-aged lady in uniform rose to the occasion and her kind face reminded me of Southern hospitality.

"Sì, please, a taxi," I managed to get out without slurring.

The taxi ride was a total waste of money, but I didn't trust this outfit, these breasts, and the fact I wasn't on my game in the Miami morning. A necessary expense.

"Good morning, Miss." The man at the counter of the store grinned as I walked in with three-inch stilettos. Ridiculous for the a.m. hours, but I had nothing else to wear.

Charles must have been slipping because, although his bodyguard guy relocated me and provided me some plastic to charge things on, I needed some clothes to get around in. Well, at least to get breakfast. This guy was looking at me like he would swallow me whole. Not today. If the man only knew what I could do to him and his testicles with my hands, it would wipe the smile off his greasy, sad face.

I scanned the small market and found what I wanted, hand-made chorizo and egg wrap delivered from a local restaurant that supplied many of the stores with breakfast food on this side of town. I waited until I got back to my hotel room to bite into my breakfast, and the whole annoying errand for a perfect meal was worth it. Meat, peppers, cheese, potatoes, fat. So good.

In the middle of cleaning up the small desk where I ate, I heard a light knock at the door. I put the hotel bathrobe over my dress and kicked off my shoes. I looked through the peep-hole and saw a maroon and cream uniformed bellhop holding a large white boutique box.

"Miss Vargas, a package from the front desk."

I debated retrieving my weapon—a setup always comes in a nice package—but instead grabbed a ballpoint pen. I could inflict some damage with this if it came to it. I summoned my usual adrenaline kick and opened the door. A few minutes later I was unwrapping a new set of clothes and shoes that were just what I needed.

The hotel phone rang. I answered knowing who it would be.

"You got my package, dear."

"Ya tu sabes, Charles. A little late though. I expected this earlier," I said, as my voice slipped back in time. Hearing my Borinquen-Spanglish accent back, I heard his sigh into the phone, "Don't get sloppy, dear."

He hung up, but I knew what he meant. I wasn't perfect with my Argentinian pronunciation. This was the new me, but only time would tell if the whole persona would stick. I hated that part.

I showered and changed into the clothes Charles had sent. "Don't get sloppy," I whispered under my breath as I showered the sweat off my well-toned body. Getting sloppy was exactly what I was doing, and Charles knew about each of my mistakes.

Sure, I got nostalgic every once in a while. After all, I was blackmailed into this life. But I was doing something that needed to be done. Life and death, right or wrong, good versus evil. Or at least, the greater good versus the smaller evils. I closed my eyes in the shower, letting the water run down my back. Each step I took away from Valderron and closer to my new life was supposed to lead me back to the only time I was loved unconditionally. I understood this assignment was what I was choosing for myself each day.

I trained to live another life so I could leave one behind. I made up my mind to be better. No more surprise trips to Miami or calls in the night. Paltrini had to be better in perfection or insanity. I would try harder in my new life.

Next assignment: reassure Charles and the agency that I was very much the woman for the job.

Joelle owed me a happy ending. If I couldn't have one, maybe she could. She needed to spend that money, and I wanted to see her do it. The $400,000 was half of my sign-on bonus to the agency. The money could change her life. I doubted she would spend it right away. On a secure line, which had been placed in my bag, I contacted the lawyer in charge of my formal affairs. The agency had suggested her.

"Joelle McCoy hasn't contacted me yet," Agnes Lopez said, when I asked about the money. "We met at the funeral, but she hasn't reached out."

"I didn't pay you to collect interest on my money," I said. "Call the newspaper she works at. Drive to Canton, Missouri yourself. See that she gets that money, or I will collect a refund myself."

"Of course. Consider it done."

She worked closely with Aquila and she knew how important it was that my loved ones were taken care of.

Jimm and Chantrea received the other half of the bonus money. They took a big risk taking in the daughter of two agents, and I wanted to repay their kindness and courage in any way I could. They would always have a special place in my heart.

Valderron got nothing except the memories. I shuddered at the thought of some other woman spending my money. That would be the day!

Later that night I met Charles in an Atlanta condo owned by the agency. I stopped asking questions after Charles reminded me how dangerous it was to see how decisions were made. I wouldn't know anything above my pay grade. The interior was sparsely decorated but provided all the essentials for agents in the area. Charles had already made himself at home. He was pouring himself a sparkling water from the refrigerator. He must have something else going on after our appointment. He usually had a real drink in his hand.

"I heard you all the way down the hall, clacking away with those shoes," he said, as he lifted his glass to take a drink.

"At least you had warning. Most men never knew what hit them," I said, flashing my most dangerous grin.

I surveyed my handler. He was handsome, pretty, a youthful baby face but firm enough to never be mistaken for anything other than a man. Six-foot-two inches tall with a tight body. A nice pair of blue eyes. I was convinced they were very well-made contacts lenses, like my own. For sure he had been under the knife, and I often wondered who he had been before this assignment.

He spoke in Sussex-accented English, high society breeding, but that meant absolutely nothing in the long run. He had trained to be the Charles that stood before me. Before training, he could have been an Aborigine who gave walkabout tours for all I would ever know. He was formal enough on all occasions for me to assume he might actually be European. I didn't want to know. I liked the allure of mystery that came along with my handler.

We both sat down on the hard but stylish divan.

"Explain to me, just for fun, how you ended up in Miami with no papers."

"Oh, it's a long boring story. You wouldn't be interested."

"Don't test me today. I already covered your ass and I deserve my due," he said. "I had to lie for you, gorgeous."

Charles noticing my body and complimenting me gave me a small glimmer of hope. Did he lie about being gay the first time I approached him with the idea of us getting together? Sex between agents was discouraged but so often necessary. It wasn't a career-killer.

"Oh, it was your standard; I rolled my R's and gave the guy my best Paltrini smile. He was your generic older, rich yacht owner offering a ride in from the Bahamas."

Charles gave me a disapproving nod.

"Don't give me that look. He found me, and it seemed like something a free woman on vacation from work just might do. Why don't you explain to me what you do on your vacations?"

"Well, I sure as hell don't go back to where I lived not even a year after I left. Do you understand the doubt this leaves us with? All the questions. Tell me now if this is too much for you. I do not want to hear from you or anyone else that you are in Miami."

When telling a lie, adding a bit of the truth always served me well.

"Charles, it's not too much. I just wanted to reassure myself that everyone involved stayed alive and well. People tend to disappear, and I know my former partners might not give the investigation a rest when I mysteriously died."

His cheeks blushed a bit red, but I thought I saw understanding in his eyes.

"Everyone is alive, and no one is inquiring any more than is to be expected. You have to trust me, ole' girl, because if you don't, we cannot work together. The body from the morgue we used was near identical and the team in charge of the operation is the best at what they do. They are not some local yokels as you Americans might say."

He was telling me the truth. They had done a superb job.

"Okay, Charles. Case closed. Deal...if you indulge me every now and then about my old life. Especially about how Joelle McCoy is turning out."

"Really? Your Army friend?" he said. "How American!"

"Listen, she was family to me, and she matters more than anyone else I left behind. And since you are all stringing me along about my parents, it's the least you can do."

ALICIA DILL

He didn't acknowledge the elephant in the room. Clara and Carlos. A fine-spun web of lies that had to be maintained. Someone would eventually choke on the actual truth.

"Fine, done," he said though there was something bitter behind his authority. "But I am sending you back to South America tomorrow for more work. You are slipping in too many obvious ways—presence, and tonality. You have to be you; you need an extended home visit."

Home visit meant Argentina, which was, surprisingly, a hopping CIA location. Everyone from the Italian Mafioso to Colombian drug runners appreciated the import and export market of the country and its ports. Most had money, and where money was involved, so was the agency. I liked the country well enough. Would it ever truly be my home? I couldn't picture myself feeling that way anywhere but the United States.

"Argentina? That's a heavy assignment with some buena comida," Aquila said, after I debriefed him over the phone during my Virginia training. "Your parents loved that place. It was really hopping back in the day with every type of boogie man. I think you actually stayed there a while as a kid. The timing would be right."

Did I go to Buenos Aires as a child? I remembered living in different places temporarily outside of the home base of Miami, but it was hard to grasp any of the genuine details when I was three or four years old. In my mind's eye, I could see my mother packing us up, my father smoking outside. Suitcases always ready.

"I want to play with the other kids outside," I remember asking. "How come we don't have another friend for me."

"Not part of the plan," she said, patting my shoulder. "You get to be the only special girl around here, mija."

And I was special, until I wasn't. Their absence and death put the weight of the world on my shoulders. I was in charge of my fate. And my family was what I made it. At least I had fifteen years with them. According to Aquila, my mom worked the intelligence gathering that the rest of the agency advertised as a career officer's work. The kind of job that took place online, so that it appeared the assassins didn't actually exist and the trash just took itself out. I wasn't sure exactly what my dad's job was. Why couldn't my work be out in the open? Why did my experience have to be one where there was no turning back?

As a soldier, I had a nationalistic, more than patriotic, love for where I came from and who I worked for. It was ironic that, for me to indulge in that pride, my own country required I live completely off the grid. A ghost agent. Any other way of living this life—that was how people in my line of work got themselves killed. Too proud.

An Argentinian woman named Paltrini could not, would not have my job. This was enough to keep me sane. Charles finished what he was packing in the other room and came out. He sat down next to me.

"My dear, you need something I can't give you," he said and gripped my hand in his.

I swallowed. "Peace of mind."

"No, a partner, maybe even some relief from all this pent-up energy," he said.

"Oh," I said, surprised. "Romance was not on my priority list."

"Did you hear me use the word romance? I am going to provide you with a little fun. Let's call it a test. A man you may even recognize from your time in the sandbox. He will know none of this. You better bloody convince him you are who you are supposed to be. He's a bit of a liability so if this doesn't work out, I don't want him coming back home."

"So now I'm killing Iraq vets. That's just great."

"Well, hopefully not again. Only if one of you mess it up," he said, warning me. I now understood that he knew my past. "He could be a valuable asset, at least for now. And, you know that we'll know how it's going."

He pointed to a small suitcase he wheeled in from the other room.

"You will find an extensive history to memorize for use with other agents. The longer you work with this agency, the more you must be the woman we made you to be. Convince a fellow American soldier that you are Paltrini or don't. He is AWOL from his current assignment. And you need to be patient for when Mummy and Daddy come back."

He sized me up with his hands, grazing my upper arms. My first thought was that this wasn't going to work out. I was used to working alone. But at this very moment I was lusting after a confirmed gay man. He knew the tricks to keep me guessing. Was he, or wasn't he?

"Hurry up and wait is in my blood. Bring this new guy over," I said. "I want to play some games of my own."

I readied the three-story villa for my new guest. The home was supposed to have been passed down through the legitimate Paltrini family, but fortunately the actual family had died without a known relative to pass it along to.

The agency, with much forethought, purchased it for a reasonable sum from the municipality, and I suddenly had some authenticated parentage. Those assholes even sent me on a meet and greet with the neighbors. Most were pleased to have a normal-looking tenant in their peaceful 'hood. Normalcy was my specialty. Meeting men from my past in a new identity was not. The villa was quaint, but small by comparison to the surrounding real estate. It was a palace compared to where I slept for many years of my life, but my tastes were changing as quickly as my bank account swelled. I made do with modern and tasteful furniture reminiscent of the Mediterranean styles I found in the design magazines. I wanted to bring some of the old country back into the Paltrini home.

The original family kept everything in good condition, clean and simple, if not a bit old-fashioned. When I moved in, I had two of the most important parts of the house gutted for renovation, the kitchen and the three bathrooms. Now, it looked modern in all the right places.

I would need to be a great actress if I was to convince this new partner that I was not an American soldier like he was. He may even recognize me if what Charles said was true. I hoped for his sake that he was attractive. We could live together more easily if he wasn't a complete troll.

At the market, I found a grocer's stall with fresh vegetables and an assortment of nuts. A sign explained that the beef was in the truck's cooler.

"What's fresh today, sir?" I asked the grocer. "I have a blind date."

"You have come to right place," he answered, in a slang version of Spanish I could barely understand. Patagonian maybe?

He brought out what he called a man's meal. And I paid him handsomely for it.

I bought a couple of days' worth of steaks, vegetables, and cheeses, and even some various vintages and liquors. It had been a while since I fed a grown man and, if anything, I wanted to be a decent host.

Fresh off an identity crisis, steadiness was the name of the game. All I had to do was be a normal agent and only eliminate the other person if I blew my new cover. If I did well, I might even have a partner.

Chapter Five

At a quarter to eight p.m. I heard a car coming up to the row of villas. It had to be him. My elderly neighbors didn't own a car and rarely had visitors so late in the evening. The car parked in front of my house. Showtime. I had practiced my Lunfardo accent, a mix of Spanish and Italian, throughout the day at the marketplace with the various vendors, but I couldn't ask them if I sounded legitimate. Only the coolest kids spoke like this, according to the relevant experts at the CIA, who probably stole the information searching social media.

"Excuse me Ma'am, when I ask for fresh cut flowers, do I sound authentically Argentinian?"

Of course I could pass, but then, this was a big world with lots of people. The CIA picked me, didn't they? It had to count for something. And then I was unsure again.

I took in a deep breath and smiled before I opened the door. I knew it was him, but was I ever surprised?

A sculpted, elegant man stood before me. He returned my smile and offered his hand. I grasped it weakly, forcing him to hold my fingertips. He was tall and was forced to half-bow. As I walked forward, I touched his shoulder and kissed both sides of his face.

He towered over me, but my heels gave me enough height for the gesture. He returned the air kisses and kept grinning. Kisses first, then names.

"Welcome to my home. You must be..." My voice trailed off.

"Gabriel Fieldstone, pleased to finally meet the lovely Miss Paltrini."

"Of course, you can come in and bring up what you have after you have eaten," I said.

After he stepped into the foyer, I went to close the door behind him. I paused as I realized that it was Staff Sergeant Sebastian Reeves in my home, no longer dead in a casket somewhere in the United States as I had presumed.

Charles had said he was somewhat of a liability, but how much of one? He was supposed to be deceased. In Iraq, I was there when he came back to the camp in a body bag.

"There wasn't much left of him after the blast," the chaplain said, as we stacked his weapon on a pair of his desert-colored boots and played Taps.

The bugler's song rang in my ears and my fingernails dug into my palms. I now had living proof the agency was creating its own army, one that had no ties to home. But now, instead of Reeves, I had to remember him as Gabriel Fieldstone.

Unclenching my fists, I decided to adapt. I turned around, a little lighter in my heels, a little happier because of who was standing in my house. When Charles told me I would recognize him, I thought about who I would have wanted to see again. I considered the many men I'd happily kill just to avoid putting up with their annoying characteristics or worse. Some of those soldiers were responsible for my nightmares, and on a really bad day, I would say they were to blame for my current employment. On a good day, a day I counted my money, I would still suffer with those fighters here. Men who made me hard, pushed me past the point of saving, past the point of hoping for a normal life.

I escorted Fieldstone to the kitchen and then the dining room to show him the fabulous spread I prepared for him. He still seemed surprised at his surroundings, and maybe he was checking me out from behind.

"I'd like to freshen up and shower before dinner, if that's fine with you. I don't want the food to get cold," he said, and then smiled. I had warming plates under everything hot, and the steaks, simply salted, were still soaking in their juices.

"Of course, Mr. Fieldstone, the bathroom is to the right and across this hall." I gestured for him to follow me. "This is your room. You can feel free to, how do you say, make yourself at home."

I could have pretended to struggle more with English, but we both knew I had to be the best if we were working for the agency. I had to remember to keep him guessing about who I was. He could never know the truth. And I anticipated he would be okay with that.

He went back to his rental sedan and unloaded a small single suitcase. He packed light. I wondered how Charles had briefed him about me.

A few minutes later, I heard the shower turn on. Sergeant Reeves had always been quiet around me when we served together. He was a squad leader in an infantry unit. I recalled some of the basics about him, not because he had ever said more than two words to me while we were deployed together, but from what was said after his falsified death. I guessed he was around thirty-two or thirty-three years old by now. His father was in Iraq when he died and had been a possible shoe-in for adjutant general of both the Air and Army National Guard, I remembered, in New Mexico, maybe Arizona.

Reeves was married but I didn't think he had children. So, he made some poor young woman a widow before her time? The rest of the story he would have to tell me himself. It might be challenging to get him to speak to me but maybe he would open up to Paltrini.

He had no words for Chapa, but at the time he was a married man, and that was more than appropriate, honorable even. I couldn't tell him about my past so it shouldn't matter.

As I listened to the shower running, a little part of me hoped Reeves—now Fieldstone—could be a companion to me in the many ways I needed. I was getting ahead of myself. The thoughts of his fake death confused me. Per usual, I considered unraveling.

I considered calling Aquila for a familiar voice but thought better of revealing the agency's secrets. He was no doubt still greasing the wheels of justice, and I was in Argentina no longer under his command. I found in him a link to my family and my past.

I busied my hands with preparing a quick salad to follow our main meal. I could at least feed the man before I made any more decisions.

Awkwardly, we sat down to dinner almost an hour after he arrived. He wanted to unpack all his gear before eating. I reheated everything in the oven, a gesture to show that I cared about it tasting good. By the time we ate, it was dark outside, and I was almost too hungry to eat like a lady. I usually ate standing over the sink because it became too much effort to clean the dishes when it was just for one person. I didn't need to remind myself how I was loneliest during mealtimes.

After a few minutes of mannered conversation about his trip and the food, Fieldstone surprised me by reaching across the table and touching my wrist.

"Thank you, Miss Paltrini, for treating me and hosting me in your home. I haven't had a meal like this in a long, long time," he said, as he gazed thoughtfully at me across the table built for six.

What had he been eating? Where was he before Argentina and what made this an ideal assignment for him? Charles must have slipped in a photo of me. I had to accept what my appearance did to the male brain. It cost a fortune.

In this moment I ached to call Charles and demand a full-fledged report on this guy. I was used to getting everything summed up in a nice, neat package. But a call would only serve to heighten Charles's curiosity about our meeting.

It was a whirlwind two days of running into the city and getting to know each other through training and briefings. Charles wasn't at these meetings, and I was surprised. We were clearly both on thin ice with the people assisting us. They provided little information beyond background research on our location and providing us with each other's cover details, which we memorized. It seemed like we were waiting for something we didn't know about yet. The assassin is the tail that wags the dog. No real work until it's time.

Later, the evening of our second full day together, I decided I wanted to find out more about Gabriel Fieldstone the old-fashioned way. The reason was very simple. I needed to detach myself completely from my old life. Sgt. Reeves, now Gabriel, hadn't taken a second look at Concepcion Chapa. The plastic surgery wasn't something I ever wanted. I assumed I would age naturally, and I was fine with the wrinkles and the softness I saw other women carrying. I was a warrior, a strong female, a Valkyrie. When I sat with the doctor who burned off my fingerprints, I understood. The new nose, the new jaw, the new fakeness wasn't easy to grasp.

I read online about the emotions involved in changing one's appearance. I wasn't going to be okay about it for a long time. The worst part was how much more I looked like a true South American woman with an artificial makeover to make my every feature desirable. I was an imposter in my own skin. My birth mark remained on my left calf. This was my link back to myself. After my second mission, I stared at the small shape that resembled a postage stamp for hours. A lot for Sofia Paltrini, a little for Concepcion Chapa. I smiled thinking that Joelle McCoy would always have thousands of reminders of her identity, with all of her freckles.

I needed to get out of my head. That's where the trouble started.

"So, what do you know about me?" I asked, deciding to be bold with my questions. I did have the upper hand here. This was my home.

"Oh, not much. Really, I wasn't sure what to expect. I felt nervous standing there at your door when I first arrived," he said. That surprised me. His answers rang true, giving me a little hope.

"I know that you work for my government, and you came to us from the Argentinian military. I heard you were making quite a name for yourself within the agency, something about running very tight, squared-away, solo missions. I just keep asking myself how they didn't find you sooner."

"I'm impressed that you're impressed. But I could ask you the same question, Mr. Fieldstone," I answered.

He nodded but didn't answer my question right away.

"Oh, I'm not that formal. Please call me Gabriel," he said.

I decided not to press him on where he had been before he came to my doorstep.

"Fine, Gabriel. But, Fieldstone—isn't that a bit obvious? You seem a bit more exotic than an old Anglo-Saxon name implies."

I knew the answer to my own question, but he didn't know it.

I took a deep breath, as if I were impatient—a breath like that is one of the best tells when you're trying to gain information from a person, or a suspect.

"The short answer is my mother is Southeast Asian and my dad is an old American white guy," he replied.

"So, where do you come into the picture?" I asked.

"Take a guess about where they met. My age is just right for it," he said. "They met during the Vietnam War, but they weren't married until later on."

With just a few sentences, Gabriel was like an open book here at the dinner table. I hadn't gathered this much information in nine months in the desert. I kept myself from thinking too much about the Fieldstone from my Army days because this door opening into my former life, let other thoughts about myself in, too. Bad thoughts, crazy ideas, and then I was back to not sleeping and drunk dialing my former fiancé from twenty minutes away. I wasn't her anymore. I was a new person, Paltrini to the world, to Charles, to Fieldstone and to anyone else I would meet, even Joelle McCoy.

"Well, Gabriel, I would be interested to hear the long version sometime. And I assume we will have more time than discuss it. Charles told me you would be accompanying me on a few trips and staying here indefinitely. An extremely vague mission, but is this what you understood?"

"Yes, something like that. But Charles didn't tell me you would be so...." he paused, and his eyes darted to the corner of the dark stained table. I waited for it. I knew what he wanted to say, but was he blushing? Could I even tell if he was? Yes, he was blushing.

"...so beautiful. *Fotografia di belleza,* as your countrymen would put it."

I looked into his light grey eyes, brilliant against his brown skin with yellow undertones. He was a picture of beauty himself. He must have assumed I was younger than he was, and with my new plastic face and shapely body, I was. I was made to be this woman. I decided to be her. I would be his only memory of Buenos Aires or, better yet, "Miss Porteños," spicy, sexy, and passionate.

I got up from my chair, and I registered his surprise as I pulled him back from the table and sat down on his lap. His arms fell to the sides, like a whipped old man getting a lap dance, too scared to touch what he wanted. I grabbed his hands and placed them on my hips. Before he could decide what to do next, I kissed his lips, still red from the wine. He tasted like alcohol, but something else mixed in. He tasted authentically man. His lips against mine and then his tongue pressing against my mouth. He wanted to be inside my mouth.

I changed positions and, holding on to the back of his neck, straddled his lap a little tighter against his awakened erection. I took the moments of adjusting to kiss behind his ear and nibble on his earlobe. He smelled like soap. I kicked off my shoes I could move on his lap more easily.

Gabriel let out a small grunt of satisfaction as the friction of our kiss moved me against his crotch. I told myself to keep control—hell I started this—but he wanted to finish it. I could feel his hands pull on me in the sexiest of ways. His hands mounded the flesh of my ass and hips and moved all the way up to my heaving breasts. The back of his closely cropped hair in my fingers had me wanting more. His scent was intoxicating. This was a man like no other. I closed my eyes to drink him in. My muscles tensed as he massaged underneath my blouse.

Did I plan on any of this happening? Concepcion Chapa was somewhat of a good girl when it came to the right time to sleep with a man, but ultimately her way didn't matter anymore. Charles must have seen this coming and was more than likely surveilling us on a video camera somewhere. He preferred men but this would turn on any human being with a pulse.

Gabriel wasn't disappointing me, at all. He loosened my shirt and bra and I was more than happy to let him do so. He continued to kiss me with a slow burning passion. My finger dug into his hardened shoulders, and I grabbed whatever I couldn't see. He was so well built, I wanted him to bring me pleasure.

He was no stranger to a woman's body. He didn't know anything about me I considered personal, yet this connected us. He lifted me off him, and in one strong swoop he brought me to his chest and carried me to the guest room, his room, for now. It was the closest, and I didn't care where he fucked me, as long as he did so immediately. He placed me roughly on the bed and took off his shirt. He appraised my body, and his approval was immediate. His eyes must have seen a desperate woman, naked on top with her skirt pulled over her ass.

He pulled his dark blue jeans over his firm muscled ass and leaned over my bare legs. I reached up to pull him close but decided against it. I surprised him with a hard slap against his smooth cheek. His eyes widened in disbelief. He licked his lips instead and gingerly touched the place where I just assaulted him. Before I could decide what to do next, he grabbed my wrist and held my arms to my sides. He was silent as he worked. I had wanted to test his will, and he seemed not to mind my little love tap.

I wriggled to get my arms free. It only made things hotter. I couldn't even fake wanting to be rid of him because I was grinning against my will underneath his weight.

Gabriel locked eyes with me and placed his knee between my legs. They fell open with the slightest urging. I needed this. Whatever it was. He bent down and released my hands. I tried to move back after being set free, but his tongue was there. My hands bent to lift his head off me. It was intense. I could not endure. I wanted my control back, but he had me writhing in pleasure. He still held my wrists, so he used every bit of his mouth and my mind went completely blank.

He released my hands and sat up on the bed, watching my every move, gauging my reaction to what he just did to me. He grabbed his jeans and shirt and began redressing himself.

I couldn't move; I wanted to cry out. I managed to sit up on the bed and I slapped him again. I was beginning to like this new side of myself. It worked well, slapping him. Before I knew it, my own cheek was stinging from his retaliation.

I was ready for him. I needed him inside me to give him something back from myself. My essence.

He grabbed my wrist and flipped me on my belly. I was ready for him. He entered slow, teasing the outside of me. He was all the way inside. I buried my head into the pillow. This was how I needed to be taken. This was the pounding I needed deep inside to silence all other thoughts, dreams. Alive after being dead for so long. Gabriel finished without warning and he collapsed on top of me. His sheer size made me feel heavy but secure. Whoever I was in this moment, she was going to rest easy tonight.

And I did sleep, a bit easier than previous nights.

Gabriel was a man of equal tenacity in bed. His silent acknowledgment of our sharing the bed made me second guess staying, but when he held me close to his chest and settled into sleep, I closed my eyes and took everything he was offering. No nightmares, no dead bodies slept with me for the entire night. I could let the paranoia about Gabriel creep in, but I decided to act against my nature and do something a little dangerous, be vulnerable instead of my usual hardened self.

The next morning, I awoke before him, and I beamed considering this fact. Throughout the night, he slept with one arm on my pillow and the other arm across his well-muscled chest. He was a sight. Solid, practically hairless, and a warm-blooded human being. My standards mirrored those of a vampire after such a long drought of intimate contact.

I tiptoed from his room barefoot and completely naked. It was a freeing way to travel. Of course, I had been naked around my house, but it wasn't after a long night of passionate lovemaking and restful sleep.

How could two ghosts sleep so completely together? I should have called Charles at some point, but I didn't want to share this encounter yet. I wished I could call Joelle to hear her thoughts. Even the dull ache of our shared past wasn't on my mind. I didn't notice any imperfections last night. If they were there, I would find them later.

I cleaned the plates from our dinner, and then I prepared us breakfast. My family wasn't big into eating right when waking up. But the military ingrained in me the importance of the first meal of the day. It might in many circumstances be the only meal I ate before a mission, so I learned to fuel myself like a well-oiled machine.

I made scrambled eggs and toast; I had already gone through two cups of coffee before he came into the kitchen wearing briefs.

"Good morning, Miss Paltrini," he said, his voice still scratchy from sleep.

I turned to protest him calling me miss, but his arms were around my waist. He kissed my shoulder. I wore a set of shorts and tank top pajamas. So, he had enjoyed himself. Of course he had. He looked positively edible in the morning light coming in from the bay window of the dining room. If Charles had handpicked Gabriel for me, he had exquisite taste in men. And why wouldn't he?

We ate in silence though he looked up occasionally from his meal and nodded in appreciation. Was he thinking the same things about me? Was he thanking the agency for bringing him to me? I wanted it to be true. He would have to work out because the only liability I could foresee with us was how quickly all of this was happening. Concepcion Chapa knew better than to trust anyone, under any circumstances. Now, Gabriel Fieldstone was unravelling the latest version of me. The kind of disorientation that makes it hard to work. Did I have a choice in all this? Only time would tell.

Chapter Six

FOR THE NEXT SEVERAL WEEKS GABRIEL AND I WERE INSEPARABLE. He had the impossible habit of letting me lead him around, except in the bedroom. And I was sure some poor sucker was out buying new memory cards for all the surveillance Charles was probably doing on us in the sack. He did seem like the voyeur type.

Gabriel liked our arrangement. After all, this was supposed to be home for me, and the longer he stayed, the more it became our place. When we went shopping, he brought his own credit card for the purchases. He didn't even blink at the cash register. If I had had a girlfriend, I would have told her all these amazing details. If we wanted something, we bought it. Concepcion Chapa would hate Sofia Paltrini and the gross use of taxpayer funds. My career with the CIA dictated that I enjoyed my lifestyle because there was nothing else but killing people. Not until my parents showed up, or the real reason behind this charade was revealed.

If I died, I was sure the U.S. government would get the money in my bank account, not Joelle. I couldn't send another check. It would put her through my death twice, and who wants blood money. And if Joelle ever found out what I did for the money, it would just make it worse. Let her enjoy the $400,000 relatively guilt free. "Hey buddy, here is a couple of millions of dollars, I only killed a few guys for it so go buy yourself something nice."

With both of us at the top of the agency food chain, we ate and shopped in the best places Buenos Aires had to offer. The city was known as the Paris of South America. I didn't particularly enjoy Paris, but it was sweet when Gabriel told me about it and then held my hand in public. I told myself it was part of the cover, and it was. Paltrini got her hand held, not Chapa.

That afternoon we were meeting Charles at an apartment a few miles outside of the city. We had spoken a few times over the phone, but our handler didn't ask too many questions.

Gabriel spoke to me about how he'd arrived in Buenos Aires, as if preparing for the possibility we would be separated after our meeting with Charles. I hadn't pushed him for any information because I didn't want to get tangled up in my own web of lies, because that's what they were, lies. He admitted he'd had a privileged childhood as the son of an Army officer. But his mother's influence kept him grounded. He was an only child and wanted to make his parents proud.

"I think they loved each other more than they loved being parents. But maybe that's the best way—that they loved each other more."

His words clicked in my brain. My own parents must have felt that way, to leave their teenager. The familiar refrain started up again. Specifically, because they were both always trying to do the right thing, focused on their duty and obligation. They loved me, but I wasn't the reason for their existence either. I wasn't planned. I considered the idea and silently agreed. I always loved kids, but I wasn't going to have any of my own. Romantic love would be the only type of love I experienced.

It was Gabriel's mother who worked with the CIA as a young teenager. This detail meant the CIA seemed to be activating the offspring of its current or former agents. There was probably a larger conspiracy related to that revelation, but I was not tempted to dig.

"Do you want to know more?" he asked, tentative and searching my face in the dimly lit bedroom. He was cautious and caring like that.

"Are you kidding me?" I said. "Of course I want to know more. I promise I can keep a secret," I said with a wink.

"The short version is still long, but I've only told a few people. It is a very romantic story, you know."

I was anxious to hear it, but I sulked a bit when he said he'd told a few people, most likely his former wife. Chantrea and Jimm came from the same region as his mother, and I knew them to be kind, but a bit guarded about their past.

We held hands as he continued to tell his story. I huddled closer to him as he spoke close to my ear.

"My mom comes from a group of people called Tai Dum, who aren't really from just one country. In fact, you can find them in Vietnam, Laos, Thailand, Cambodia, and even Southeast China. They have migrated throughout the years because of the usual stuff, persecution and war."

I nodded for him to continue.

"My mother's father helped out the French side and the family was living in Laos. Eventually, the Communists killed him, but my family still lived well in the area. They learned to speak French and a little English."

He was animated speaking about his family, and I could tell it must be hard to be separated from his parents.

"My mom began working with family members who supported the French and later the United States efforts during

Vietnam. She carried notes in her schoolbooks and left them with a young American lieutenant who served as another runner. She was followed several times, but she was smart and would always evade the soldiers.

I shifted on the bed, trying to picture what his mom would look like as a schoolgirl.

"The lieutenant was so enamored by this girl who brought him such confidential information, but in the beginning, he couldn't allow his feelings to interfere with their mission. When the war was winding down, he decided to risk it one afternoon and wrote her a letter in English. She couldn't understand everything in the letter, but she did realize the letter was meant for her and from the lieutenant. She recognized the English word *love*. That man was my father."

He was finished, but I still had so many questions.

"So, how did they leave Laos together?"

"They didn't. Many members of her family were killed as the war continued. The agency got her a flight out of the country with some other upper-class citizens because of the risks her family had taken."

"So, where did she go?"

"Her sisters went to France, but she decided to try her luck in the United States and to find my father."

"But, why wouldn't they stick together? Couldn't they have gone with her?"

"There were more opportunities in France for her family, because by this time they all spoke French, and there was a history from colonization that tied the region together. She flew to the United States and reunited with my father where his family lived in Arizona. She was pregnant in the first month of them being together. They really loved each other."

"She must have been very beautiful, your mother."

"Oh, she still is," Gabriel said. "She seems twenty years younger than she is and runs five miles every day."

I wanted to get more personal with Gabriel, but I didn't want to shut him down.

"Do your parents know you are here?" I asked, rolling back onto my side to face him.

"Yes and no," he replied.

"What does that mean?"

"It means they know I am with the agency, but they don't know where I am. They said it's enough for them because they understand this life. My dad is the one who kind of suggested it."

"Really, why would anyone want this life for someone they love?" I said, as I tried to push away the thoughts of my own parents contemplating my life choices. It was much easier to throw stones than to dodge them.

"It's more complicated, Sofia."

He seemed to enjoy calling me miss, but after I insisted, he was finally calling me Sofia.

"He just saw something in me after I came home on leave. His work with all the government agencies gave me some different opportunities to do something more important than urban combat in the middle of a shit storm."

"You were different, how?" I asked, noting the sweat forming on his brow.

This was getting too close to the truth for me, but did he

think like me? I had to know. It couldn't be so easy. I had my own bad dreams to deal with, and I was sure he had his.

"I don't want to scare you, woman. I guess it's best to say I saw too much to go back to my life," he said. "It made me a perfect candidate to do my job in a smarter way for a lot more money.

"My dad was too smart for his own good, but he made the military work for him. It's different now, and the Army isn't the only game in town. In fact, before this I was set up to be a civilian mercenary. I felt like I got an offer I couldn't refuse. I had too much responsibility and no authority over my own life. I'm a coward for leaving a wife behind, I know it. It's better for us. That is what I tell myself at least. She is a war hero's widow instead of a lonely, miserable young woman with her husband gone all the time."

I knew I should just stop pushing him, but I couldn't hold back the questions.

"Do you miss her, Gabriel?" I asked.

He looked in my eyes, and I saw the sadness in him. And the anger.

"Don't ask me that. In fact, no more questions tonight," he said.

I leaned in and kissed Gabriel with everything I could give him of myself. I wanted to comfort him with my body.

"Buenas noches, Gabriel."

"Good night," he said, as he kissed my forehead and turned to face the other wall. If it was all true—and I hoped it was—he was truly laid bare, and he had allowed me to know him more intimately.

He hadn't asked me any of those questions, and part of me knew I should have stopped.

Sometime during the night, we came back together and made love. I slept until he woke me up by removing the Egyptian cotton sheet wrapped completely around me.

We had another meeting with the boss man. Like any other job, it was all about meetings.

Waiting in a safe house, Charles explained that this particular apartment overlooking the busy commercial district in Montserrat would be our go-to place if for some reason we could not go back to the villa. It was small but nicely decorated. There was no comparison to our current living quarters, but it fit the bill for safe-house material.

"Are you ready to play ball?" Charles asked.

"Yes, with the two of us together, we would be unstoppable, you know," I added with a slight smile. If memory served me correctly Gabriel was an expert marksman, and we usually played with unarmed, unsuspecting individuals who we found at their most vulnerable state.

"Do we get to play as a team, all of us? Or are you going to join us this time, Charles?" Gabriel asked.

"I'll stay back of course. You know I don't get my hands dirty, Gabriel. That's her job," Charles replied.

Yes, leaving the killing up to the lioness. Not the lion.

"I am ready when you gentlemen are," I said, feigning a yawn.

"Okay, you will be traveling separately but here are your means of contact. No text messages, not a bloody wrong number, just essential communications," Charles said as he handed us our new cell phones. Nothing special, just burners. Most likely so we would have a separate GPS on hand. The CIA didn't take make land navigation skills as essential as they once were.

Charles handed us both identical folders. Once the folders were in our hands, the job officially started. No going back.

I scanned my targets. I couldn't get a solid read on any of them until I was back home, but they looked like hoods, gangsters.

"Husband and wife team, but don't mistake either one of them as less dangerous than the other. She has her criminal enterprise with drugs and prostitution. He runs guns from our favorite Nigerian drug lord. A marriage made in hell. They are both British citizens, but we have the okay because all other means have been exhausted. MI6 failed. We took this one as a favor, and to flex a little muscle. What have we got that my countrymen do not have? You two of course. I want you to do this one at a time, nice and slow. They're rarely seen together, and anyway, together would mean more guards. Here is the rest of your necessary items," he said, as he handed Gabriel a couple of security passes, a hotel key, and a memory stick for us to review later.

Something about having Gabriel with me made me a bit more confident than I should have been. These were bad people; they had to understand this was the way it would end for them. We were going to kill them, the full weight of the U.S. government for the Brits. They pissed someone off.

"Okay, children, I am leaving you to it. Here are the keys to the store. Do not come here unless it's an emergency. And if you need to come here for any other reason, make sure to inform me beforehand because we do have an alarm and video surveillance on the outside. Do not use it as an additional storage area for all that excessive stuff you keep buying. How much rubbish could you possibly need?" Charles said, smiling.

Gabriel tried not to blush, but I could tell he was embarrassed. I expected it. Charles was always all up in my shit. That was his job after all.

But Charles had a calming demeanor, and his surveillance of my activities didn't bother me. He was careful because I hadn't been able to say for sure where he was watching me from. He probably used one of his boy toys to do the footwork while he shopped for himself.

"Okay, Charles. We get it, you're onto us, we wouldn't have it any other way," I said. Just for fun I winked at Gabriel. "You did put us together so I should address it. But I won't."

"Of course, Agent Paltrini," he said and nodded to Gabriel and slipped out the door.

We surveyed the apartment. There was cash and a small arsenal of weapons in the black cases in the back closet. A small key opened all cases. The kitchen was stocked with non-perishable food items. I considered stealing a jar of marinated artichoke hearts to pair with dinner later but decided against it. What if it was the last remaining food item for some unlucky person who needed the place?

We left twenty minutes after Charles. The ride back to the villa was quiet. Gabriel seemed to be concentrating on something while he drove. I appreciated his silence and imagined what we would look like to someone on the outside world, an inconspicuous car, a black Honda Accord, believable for our age. We still looked a little like outsiders, but no amount of training could make us completely invisible.

Gabriel was hard to forget. He could have been from many different places around the Eastern Hemisphere. Possibly even Latin American, something like a mix between an indigenous person and a European.

Argentina was a melting pot of sorts, just like home. He might be a liability because he hadn't had plastic surgery since he crossed over into the dark side of things. Anyone from his past would recognize him on sight, especially his eyes. They were like windows to the soul, and in Gabriel's case, stained glass windows, beautiful in color and shape. They were striking but it could be his Achilles heel in this line of work. Thinking about it, why did I have to change my appearance so completely?

We arrived back at the villa. Our fortress, as Gabriel called it, because of its high iron gates. In a seemingly safe neighborhood, the Paltrini family must have prepared for the worst.

We had twenty-four hours to prepare for the mission; I needed more than that, but Charles was testing us by not giving us plenty of time for solid planning.

After reading the file, Gabriel suggested we take the husband out first. I looked at the five bodyguards assigned to the husband, but apparently there was a big club soccer match at the same time as our assassination was scheduled, and they wouldn't all be there. All looked a little scary but not too bright. I noticed one of their tattoos looked like it was spelled incorrectly, unless he wanted to say NO FEAT in English instead of No Fear. What was that? An Ed Hardy shirt? That sealed the deal. We were taking him out.

I hadn't done a job for several months. Gabriel was seasoned enough, and he took the lead on all the planning. He seemed to know what he was doing, and I relaxed after a couple hours of watching him work. He barely spoke and, out of boredom, I went and fixed him a coffee.

No matter how much planning we did, something would go wrong. It happened every time no matter the length of preparation. Usually, my mistakes were easier to hide because ultimately the goal was to take out the target. The hardest job was for the analyst, gathering intelligence without tipping off the target. To limit my mistakes, I over-planned the big steps: entry, performing the kill, staging and disposal, and, most importantly, the exit. Good plans could go to shit at any one of these steps. It brought me back to my Army days. My drill sergeant used to say, "Today, somewhere in the world, someone is training to kill you." No truer words were said.

Our intelligence told us that the couple had been seen near the Punte del Este in the city of Maldonado, on the Southern coast of Uruguay. The location was perfect for all of the big steps, especially disposal.

In fact, I usually did minimal staging when I worked alone. I let the rest of Charles's team members do that part for me. Other agents insisted on having their own people do it or even staged the body themselves. I was green enough to not care; maybe when I was older and more paranoid I would.

The couple were booked at a beachside hotel, but surveillance showed this was a front and they would be separated.

The slum seemed a fitting place for them to slither down to at the end of the day. Our plan was to interrupt the husband's business transaction in a big way. Gabriel was going to be his hotshot buyer of a load of antitank missile launchers, though the deal was set up through a turned employee of the couple. "Turned" meant "paid off" and was the currency that could buy us into anywhere we wanted to go. The weapons alone would be worth more than our payment of a half million for each kill. We could split a million for both. Our plan seemed basic enough. I would be able to use one of my favorite weapons on the couple.

We packed our gear and loaded it into the Honda. Later, we would switch vehicles mid-route, but for now everything fit in the ample trunk space.

At the last minute, I remembered my motion sickness tablets for the long car trip. I always got carsick when someone else wanted to drive. How domestic of me.

Chapter Seven

Traffic was light on the outskirts of Maldonado, but once we reached the city, we ended up battling through a lunch-time rush hour. It was a day after we'd left Buenos Aires. The trip was uneventful, but the scenery was breathtaking.

As we drove by the shores of Punte del Este, I checked the road to make sure we were heading to the docks. It was a perfect spot for an arms dealer to conduct business. The targeted couple owned a warehouse only a few miles from one of the major tourist spots in Uruguay. According to the file, it was just one of the holding facilities used in their enterprise.

We passed the warehouse so as not to arouse suspicion.

"Did you see the BMW sedan parked out front?" I asked, while I scanned the license plate files to compare to our case notes.

"I have seen about a hundred cars just like it, but to answer your question, I did take note," he said.

"Got it, I was just checking. It's been a while, and I'm not used to doing this with a partner," I said. I thought about Joelle. She was more than a partner, and she was the only person I'd trusted up until this point. I had to wait and see with Gabriel.

He took his hand off the gearshift and squeezed my thigh.

"I know, sorry about my tone," he said. "I can be an asshole sometimes. My last partner was a double agent, so you can guess how that turned out for him. I was thinking about that while we drove. You are nothing like that though."

"Apology accepted," I said.

We parked near another storage place nearly a half mile down from the target's warehouse.

"Do you need help with any of your gear?" he said, gesturing toward the trunk where my sniper rifle was held in a pink suitcase.

"No, I don't," I said. "I can wheel a suitcase." Since Army basic training...

Nearly two hours after we parked, I was set up behind my sniper's rifle, the H-S Precision Pro Series 2000 HTR used by the Israeli military.

My hip buzzed, and I saw it was an unknown number. It rang just once and then my screen went black. I'd expected this signal from Gabriel at least twenty minutes ago, but he must have run into trouble.

He had the harder job out of the two of us, because his kill would be up close and personal. I needed to be technically accurate. He needed to be fast.

I closed my eyes, slowed my breath. I opened my eyes to use my external ballistic calculator. It quickly factored the wind, altitude, temperature, and my elevation shooting through a busted-out window of a lighthouse.

My goal was to take out Colonel Oliver Williams and Gabriel would take out any remaining associates, with me providing cover. I would not be able to take out multiple targets with assured accuracy at this distance in the time we had to pull this off. I also had to completely miss my partner.

Gabriel approached the spot where he and Williams were supposed to meet to discuss working together.

Williams was a small man with a shock of white hair. He

commanded the audience surrounding him, but, meeting a first-time client with only two associates—what an amateur.

I watched as Gabriel stepped to the man's right while they spoke, and I knew now was the moment.

I held my breath, and in the space of that second, I squeezed the trigger slowly and with purpose.

I exhaled and brought the binoculars to my face.

The colonel was lying on the ground next to one of his associates.

Where was Gabriel? I scanned the area, but I still couldn't see him. Three minutes passed without sight of my partner or the other associate. Did we have a runner?

Once I packed up the gear, I headed down the long steps of the lighthouse.

"Calm, calm, calm, be calm," I whispered. My heartbeat boomed in my ears. I imagined slowing down an old-fashioned timepiece. This exercise was supposed to help take control of my adrenaline.

The possibilities of Gabriel out there alone with a target made me start to feel something I didn't want to experience. The emotion was much too strong for the calculated person I had to become.

I pushed open the large, creaking door to the lighthouse.

Crack! The sound of a bullet whizzing by my ear.

I fell back onto the suitcase I'd been dragging, hitting the ground hard in the fall.

Another crack echoed in the walls of the lighthouse, but I was already down.

"Are you hit?" I heard Gabriel yell into the lighthouse.

"No, but I am down," I said, relieved to have him nearby.

He pushed through the door and picked up my twisted body, half on the suitcase and half on the floor.

"I caught the shooter; he came to find the sniper," Gabriel said, his breath choppy from running.

"Are you hurt?" I asked, searching his face for any trace of pain.

"Not me, I almost thought he got you though and I wasn't fast enough," he said.

We exited the lighthouse and I saw the motionless body of a young kid face up. He was shot in the back and the blood was soaking through his chest.

"You just caught up to a teenager, I think you were fast enough," I said, trying to assure him.

"That's good enough for me."

The shots would alert the police, but we planned to leave the scene immediately and head out for the wife. If we waited too long, she would go into hiding and we would lose our half-hour advantage. Gabriel disposed of our tools and came jogging up to the car; I was already at the wheel. He looked calm and collected in his running shorts and Under Armor short-sleeved shirt. It was big on him and I wondered if he had lost weight.

"Need a ride?" I said out the open window.

"From you? Yes, please," he said.

I drove through the bustling city and, during a lull in traffic, I decided we should switch places.

"Gabriel, can we switch drivers?

"But you were doing so well..." he said, with a smile. "How is it that you operate a high-powered sniper rifle, but you can't handle all these gears?"

"I didn't say I couldn't do it, I just said I didn't want to." The truth was when I drove with a passenger, I remembered all the movies where the driver dies the worst death. Better to be a passenger.

"Oh, you're right," he replied. "You don't want to try."

Once I settled into the passenger seat, Gabriel put his hand on my thigh while he focused on pedestrians walking right into traffic. It was a clean job, but mistakes were made on both our parts. I was still wired from my brush with death. Firing on all cylinders.

We had an hour or two before someone would come upon the bodies and alert the wife. Gabriel drove to the wife's hideout only a few streets away in a beachside bungalow. We set up in the neighboring homes on the opposite side of the street and waited.

All we needed was for the target to leave out the side entrance. There was one other point of exit, but the agency had eyes on her from a yacht anchored in the water. We worked alone yet supported. We had a whole other team that we rarely met. I think they wanted to keep the assassins away from the long-term surveillance teams.

According to the file, the target Fatima Williams was a second-generation Brit. Her parents came from a wealthy clan in Pakistan that made its fortune in the Toot region after selling its substantial natural gas holdings. She was, by all accounts, smart and beautiful, with a taste for the good life. When her parents disowned her for marrying outside the clan, Fatima was determined to continue living her lavish lifestyle no matter the cost. She might have been even worse than her husband. Her fingers were in the Afghan narcotics racket. She had no scruples about who she did business with. Thus the need for Gabriel and me.

The United States government could forgive a drug dealer, but not one with terrorist ties. Unless the U.S. was pulling the strings, and the outcome assured.

It was nearly evening when Williams came out with two young female associates.

After I confirmed through binoculars that it was Fatima, I took a deep breath, aimed, and fired in the center of her small chest. It was decided by Charles that we couldn't risk killing anyone but the leaders first. To my right, Gabriel used an altered M-16 to take out the rest of the crew. We cleared up our brass and wiped the area clean.

We spent the rest of our evening holed up in a bed and breakfast outside Maldonado, massaging all the tension of our day out of one another's muscles. Release, and then Gabriel gave me something else that bundled them all up again. I needed every bit of him, ideal, silent but deadly.

Two days after our mission, Charles called us back to the safe house. It was an important assignment, and we'd both performed well.

"First of all, I want both of you to know that I have transferred your payments to your respective accounts. I considered this a test for you, Gabriel, and I am pleased with your performance," Charles said.

Gabriel shifted in his place on the couch to relax a bit more. He expected us to do well. He looked as if he owned this couch and he was used to getting what he wanted. I thought about the option they'd given me, to kill him. What faith they both put in me, but maybe Charles gave Gabriel the same option to eliminate me.

I was reminded I was considered a liability after the stuff I pulled in Miami; Charles most likely sent Gabriel to me for the same reason. Charles probably thought if one of us did kill the other, then to the victor went the spoils.

Charles came and sat in a chair adjacent to the couch. I noticed he arrived with a couple suitcases. More targets I assumed.

"So now that we are over all the preliminaries, I want to put you both back to work," he said. "It's time for you to show off a bit. We invested hundreds of thousands into your training and you have the opportunity for some serious money. The two targets you just hit are, let's say, the top of a pyramid, and we need to work our way down through the chain. We can't give any of their other employees the chance to seize control of the operation. I suggested we bring more agents in on this, but our resources are cleaning up a huge mess in Europe. It's quite a list of characters, but you can manage. You each get twelve names, and many of the targets just need one agent on them. No one under sixteen years old, so that's a relief. Most of the targets are young and have little contact with their wives, children, etc."

Charles stood up from the chair and got two separate folders. He handed one to me and one to Gabriel.

He had mostly women and I had the guys. It would be easier that way.

"This is a young organization, so you both have an opportunity to make a real difference once it's done."

How many times had we heard the speech about making a difference? I was simply eliminating people in the name of my government, but it seemed to Charles that we had a higher calling.

"Do we have to be separated?" Gabriel asked.

"No, but I would advise it. Once you're done planning, go fast and get it done."

I scanned my list and most of them were South American names. The Williamses had really entrenched themselves in the area. They must have paid well.

Gabriel had four women on his list. Only one of them was family, a sister of the wife, Fatima.

I leaned back on the couch and took a deep breath. This was a lot at once. I was used to single targets and fast jobs. This would take a lot of effort.

"Too bad we couldn't get them all in one building and bomb it, or set off a roadside bomb. Even I could make one of those," I said.

"If it had been that easy, then we wouldn't have been called," Gabriel replied. He was right.

"The price is $25,000 for the first five and $10,000 for each confirmed kill as you get closer to the bottom of the list," Charles said. "Just so we are clear. This isn't about the money. Both of you are on a sort of salary. These bonuses in this world are not the reason to kill but we want to give you the going rate in case you are offered a better deal. We ensure we take out everyone associated so we don't have to revisit this in six months. And while you're at it, take the next week at least to study the files."

For some reason, Charles was pissing me off. I asked myself why Charles was going on about the money. I wasn't this whole different person for cash. I didn't have my face cut off to be rich. When was the part where I saw my parents? I thought back to killing a fellow soldier and my premeditated murder confession. Those threats weren't holding weight for me anymore. The only thing I could do was bide my time and try to understand the real reason I was here.

"Shouldn't we get started now?" I asked. "They might get out of the area. I know that I would."

"No, they won't leave. This is where everything is. They need to maintain this base because greed will keep them trying to take over the business. The smart ones might try it, but we have an intelligence asset monitoring the airport data globally that will make sure they can't get too far."

"Okay, but what if they don't fly?" Gabriel asked.

"Then you hunt them down. End of questions," Charles said. He seemed overwhelmed based on the wrinkled creases forming on his forehead. He looked older in those moments.

Gabriel seemed to barely register the task we had ahead of us. I didn't know him as well as I thought I did. The sex was clouding my perception of our bond. Next time, I needed a female partner, because Gabriel wasn't registering how complicated all of this could be.

I always worried first and relaxed later. I wished we would be together on this.

"You will both still share your home base," Charles said. "It's good for business that you keep up the appearances there. This could turn into a long-term arrangement."

With our instructions delivered, Charles left the apartment.

Gabriel reached across the sofa and pulled me onto the cushions. He climbed on top of me in one quick move and began kissing me like he was struggling to breathe. His hands were everywhere on my body, and I held on to whatever I could. He felt so hot. His skin seemed to be smoldering in a growing heat.

I doubted his silence was boredom.

We ended up in the bedroom, but my thoughts were racing faster than he was having me.

The room smelled of sex. I had a change of clothes in the car. Gabriel went and brought in our overnight bag as I cleaned myself up in the shower. The water was hard, but the heat was just what I needed to ease my muscles from their spasms. He was so good, maybe even a little too good to be true.

I examined myself in the mirror, messy hair and a blushed face, but beneath the exterior my eyes looked frenzied. "Maybe this is a good thing," I whispered to myself.

I wanted to think about it more. I wished I had someone I could talk about it with, but I kept everything inside, good and bad. It was the only way. I thought briefly about the list and something dropped in the pit of my stomach. Like that, my good mood was taken away. We had a week to prepare and it seemed too short. Especially with the amount of risk involved for the both of us. I was a bit more like the character I was supposed to play.

"Let's go out for dinner," Gabriel said through the bathroom door.

"Can we get something greasy and quick?" I answered. "I look like a tornado just hit my hair."

"You choose," he said.

I checked the folder of approved places to eat. A place called Artico with seafood fast food meant I could have a seafood salad, sushi and papas fritas and whatever rabas turned out to be.

"I've got the perfect place."

Chapter Eight

D<small>URING OUR DINNER</small>, G<small>ABRIEL AND</small> I <small>DISCUSSED NOTHING BUT</small> the U.S. elections. It surprised me just how passionate Gabriel became when he discussed the political debate that was currently dividing the U.S. population. He knew a lot about the way the entire government worked. He didn't need to tell me he had a degree in International Politics because many of his examples seemed thoroughly researched and thought out. I was at least able to feign ignorance, but the truth was, I never got too much into any headlines. I realized if Gabriel and I had many more dinners like this, I would need to read up a bit more on what he cared about. In this instance, Joelle would have been able to help me out. She cared about the world's problems sincerely. Like many soldiers, I usually thought about politics with much disdain. My parents were both avid readers, and, knowing what I did about their chosen careers, that was probably basic level training in the agency.

I chose to study Public Affairs because it was the only way Jimm and Chantrea would agree to support me through the Army recruitment process. Less of a chance of seeing combat. Ha! If they only knew how I turned out. The army didn't need public affairs. They needed military police. They put the rest of us on patrol and guard duty and hoped we would survive with minimal training. Jimm and Chantrea did their best the few years they had me, but the life of my real parents stayed with me.

My father Carlos was every bit an eloquent man, but he knew what it meant to be a dad. At ten years old, we went kayaking near his grandparents' village, Guayanilla in Puerto Rico. He grew up in Miami when there were few boricuas. Now, the 305 showed the popularity of Miami for other islanders besides Cubanos with almost a million strong.

"When you're out on the water, mija. You are close to me," he said. "This is where I belong. Sometimes I just wish I could have been a fisherman, like my abuelito. A better life."

"Why didn't you?" I asked. I was naïve as to why he thought a harder, manual job was the better way to go.

"Life isn't that simple. Outside of here, the world doesn't stop, and it's not as beautiful as it is here, with you."

I held onto his memory, his idea of what life could have been. When he died, I dug out the shirt he wore that day on the water. More and more of these memories were flooding through my mind as I prepared for the remote possibility of seeing them again.

And he was gone. He may have had a choice and chose to leave. That part was too much to bear. My brain couldn't decide whether it was a bad thing or a brave thing if they chose to leave me. Abandonment wasn't something I was going to work through on my own, and having those issues made me unsafe.

The restaurant was just the right combination of good food without much fuss. We could have gone somewhere nicer but this way I could focus on him and not my surroundings.

"Do you want dessert?" he asked, interrupting my thoughts.

"No, and neither do you," I quipped. Damn the chocolate cake idea. We were in training right now.

"You know you want something sweet," he said.

He motioned the waiter over and ordered flan for himself, nothing for me. I was a little disappointed not to get something too, but I knew my own limits. When the waiter brought the flan, I asked for a short coffee.

Gabriel ate his flan with such precision that I couldn't take my eyes off him. He was obviously savoring every bite.

I liked watching him indulge. It was only the night before that I'd caught him eating watermelon straight out of the refrigerator, his mouth still wet from the juice.

After we returned from dinner, Gabriel took a shower and settled in front of the computer. And so, it began. He decided he would help pull information on my targets and we would plan together. I would know precisely where he was, and I liked this.

A few hours later, we settled in on the couch and watched the local news on the new plasma screen TV in the living room. It was his most recent purchase and the one that identified him as a typical American. He insisted on satellite service and Dolby surround sound, as if I cared either way. He preferred CNN but we watched BBC.

I pondered as I laid on his lap where Joelle was and what she was doing. Every time I was remotely happy about anything significant, I had to call Joelle to talk, to share my life with her. I hoped she was finding happiness, too. She always hounded me for being ignorant and complacent about staying up on current events.

I could hear her now: "You take orders, and you never question what is behind those orders."

And I really didn't. I cared about organization and precision. Now it was costing me.

Sometime during the second hour of political commentary and entertainment wraps ups, I fell asleep on Gabriel's lap. He didn't wake me up, but I was conscious when he carried me into my own queen-sized bed.

He tucked me in and went back to the living room. I bet he would sneak another piece of watermelon when he was sure I was out. I smiled at the thought and drifted off to sleep. I awoke to a knock on my bedroom door.

"Sofia, wake up." It was Gabriel, and with a quick glance from underneath the sheets, I saw he was fully dressed. Was it really that late?

"It's one of your neighbors at the door, and she's got something for you." He appeared frustrated. "She would not leave it with me."

"Okay, I'm up. Just give me a minute."

I dressed quickly and slid a Beretta in the back of my pants. I clicked the safety off. Who knew what she wanted? I opened the door to an elderly woman while Gabriel stood out of her line of sight. She handed me a package and in rapid fire Spanish explained she signed for it yesterday while I was out.

The woman looked around the inside of my foyer, as if she wanted to come inside. Of course, she did. I had just pinpointed the neighborhood gossip hound. She had to come out sometime. I expected a visit sooner. I thanked her but decided against being hospitable, at least for now. I asked where she lived, and could I maybe come over later to thank her. Turning the tables, she could make her home ready for company.

"Of course, Miss Paltrini," she said. "It was a pleasure to meet you. I look forward to your visit."

"See you soon," I said, as I closed the door.

I knew Gabriel's grasp of Spanish was improving daily, but he looked confused trying to translate the fluid conversation. He would get it eventually, but I had a big advantage over him in that I grew up speaking both languages at home. My real parents were adamant that I master both. My mom spoke to me in Spanish and my dad in English. It was so hard for many Americans to even attempt to learn a second language. I appreciated both languages for their differences.

Gabriel did have three other languages I would have difficulty learning, Tai Dum, Thai, and Lao. He explained he spoke Tai Dum with the most ease but had to admit there was a beauty to his Thai. It was a special language, elegant in its meaning. The night before, he'd shown me a few photos of his mother that he had in his email account, and she was gorgeous, youthful and classy. I was grateful for his openness with his parents. I had little to show for my new life. He hadn't asked so I hadn't offered. That could be a sign of narcissistic tendencies, but I couldn't read people in this line of work. It used to be very easy to understand what motivated the people I worked with. Joelle was motivated by the fear of missing out. I was motivated by a sick sense of allegiance to my parents' legacy. I wasn't sure that reason would hold water much longer when my days were spent killing on a continuous loop.

After the neighbor left us, we carried the package to the living room. The shipping address was from a well-known company in Rio where I had stopped on my last trip. My hair extensions had finally arrived in all the different colors I had ordered. I didn't forget they were coming but it was a nice surprise they arrived so soon. I asked for only the best of the longest extensions possible, so it took a little effort to get exactly what I wanted from their buyer in India.

I opened the box and the handmade silk packaging reminded me that I had gone to the right place. A card was enclosed from the owner himself thanking me for my business. I was sure he appreciated it. I had ordered over $5,000 worth of human hair from him. I could have gone local, but I didn't want to do a lot of business in the city. It just made things so much simpler.

Gabriel sat down with me as I pulled the individual packets out of the box. He put his weapon on the table and got close enough to inspect my purchases.

He held a strand of strawberry blonde up to my hairline and nodded. It would be a natural-looking color if I were a Swedish runway model. I could pull it off with the right eyebrows.

I'd spent nearly two hours with the guy at a salon carefully selecting the colors I wanted. Charles had passed along the tip in case I decided wigs were not my forte. They were not. I wanted to up my game. I had used my share of wigs but no matter what I did they came off too early and didn't look completely natural.

Nothing worked for me until I worked alongside another female agent in training who told me extensions were the way to go. Almost all hair suppliers in the world went to India for their real human hair because it was the best quality, and it was cheap. The virgin strands could stand up to any chemicals in coloring and the heat of a curling iron. When I heard that I could wash the strands in the sink with normal shampoo and reuse them, I was sure about the purchase.

I went to the wide mirror in the downstairs bathroom and clipped some of the auburn strands into my hairline. The little tiny clips that secured the locks of hair were invisible. Gabriel seemed very interested in my beauty secrets.

"Oh, so now I get to have you in all these colors. Tonight, I want you to be a hot blonde. And then tomorrow, I might want the blonde again. Who knows?"

He seemed excited more about seeing me in the bedroom with my new hair than the actual practicality of it.

"Does this mean I can order some hair for you? I think you need some long, curly hair. Then you would really be a little Nikita," I said. "Or what about the Fabio look?"

"An Asian guy with curly hair and blue eyes, I could kill the targets by shock alone," he said, as he picked up some of the extensions and clipped the longest layer into his three-inch long hair.

"How do I look?" he asked, as he examined himself in the mirror. He had chosen the black hair and it flowed all the way down his back. He turned and from the front he was pretty.

"Oh my gosh, Gabriel, you look like Cher!" I said. At the mention of the name Cher, I was reminded of singing in the shower with Joelle. It seemed like a lifetime ago.

"I could grow my hair out like this. It's not just for women. Maybe a man-bun?"

"Hey, long hair is fine with me, and Charles probably already knows everything we've said, the way he watches us," I said.

"Oh really, well, let him see something else."

Gabriel picked me up and carried me to the couch cushion that wasn't covered in expensive hair extensions.

He kissed me sweetly, sat down and put my legs over his lap.

"In all seriousness, we need to take some time out of planning to get to know each other," Gabriel said as he stroked my tanned calves.

I looked into his eyes and contemplated letting him into my

head. I could spill everything and lose the accent. My reflexes kicked in and I shut that idea out as quickly as it had come. I wasn't ready, and our upcoming mission could be jeopardized. Besides, I needed to run it by Charles. After all, I still had a few unanswered questions. I was curious when he would let me know what Joelle was doing. He had said he would keep me updated.

"Is this the most targets you've dealt with in this short amount of time?" he asked, changing the subject.

"Yes, it is," I said. I was being honest about this question. How could I not be? An entire network of people would be destroyed, and Gabriel and I had a lot of work to do.

"Let's go over some of the blueprints of their newest location," he said. "It helps that these Brits are thick as thieves."

I had only loose ties with many people in my life, and I envied the targets for having a close group of people around them. They would ultimately leave this Earth together, but what more could anyone really hope for? Not to die alone seems a much better alternative.

It was a new day, but the neighbor at the door had rattled me a bit. I went upstairs to take a shower while Gabriel packed our gear. We planned to head to no man's land and zero all the different weapons. I had broached the idea of man-made bombs again to Gabriel, but he immediately said no.

"It's cowardly and it's not how I operate," he replied sternly. I agreed with him on principle, but throwing a big party and bombing it was effective.

The potential for outside civilians being caught up in the fray was what ultimately swayed me away from it. Charles wouldn't like it either, though I was sure some of the strategic bomb attacks in Colombia were our people. We just had too much to gain from the deaths of those involved. I turned on the switch on the bathroom wall linked to the hot water heater. I had just finished shaving my legs when Gabriel entered the shower with me.

"You like hot showers," he said, as he adjusted the heat.

"I guess since you're here, you can shave my back."

"Of course, I can," he said, laughing. "What about your beard?"

Our makeshift range was all business. After we spent a half hour to zero our sights, not a single round left our barrels without hitting our intended targets. He wasn't taking the sniper rifle this time. I admired that, but I had to. I was still at least 100 pounds lighter than the guys on my list, and I wanted a backup plan. Gabriel would carry a total of seven different handguns and could buy more at any black market. We would try to hold on to as many as we could but ditching the weapons was always a possibility.

It's expensive work, and I understood the massive budgets the Department of Defense dealt with every year. The taxpayers would surely understand. I mean, could we really be caught up in the business of trying to cut costs? That was the military's job. Even the FBI had resources the local police forces could only dream about. Wiretapping was not new to the CIA, but it provided us with most of the information we needed to do our job. Once the smarter criminals stopped using telephones for all their business, all government agencies turned to computer experts to track the organizations.

Many were younger than me, but their own skill sets made them irresistible to both the CIA and FBI. The one job that really hasn't fundamentally changed was the paid hired gun. Even with all the newest technology, there were only so many ways that targets can protect themselves from a bullet. We practiced extensively with moving targets and aimed for the spots a vest would not cover. Those were the "just in case" precautions.

Gabriel approached me while I cleaned my weapon.

"Do you want me to show you an easier way to get the barrel clean?"

In the military, the male soldiers were constantly trying to show me an easier way or a faster way to do something. The mansplaining was never ending in this line of work.

It just took a long time before I considered my weapon clean. I didn't know an easier or faster way; I was thorough.

"Sure," I said.

"So, what did you use with the Argentinian military?" he asked

It rattled me, but without hesitation I guessed.

"A Beretta nine-millimeter," I answered.

"Oh, then same as our military," he said.

"Yes, or maybe same as ours," I said. "The Italians do make a fine handgun if I do say so myself."

"Oh, I agree about the Italians, in general," he said. "I met a few when I was in Iraq. Good guys."

"Yes, even better that they were guys," I said, teasing his ear.

It would make everything so much easier if he knew the truth. There would be more questions, especially since he was a trained agent, and I might not always have a plausible answer.

"Do you still keep in contact with anyone from your old unit?" he asked.

"Oh yes. I have a good girlfriend from the job, but she got

out of this racket and moved to live on a farm somewhere. She's quite happy. But we are not dreaming the same dreams anymore. It makes it hard to stay in touch."

A little bit of the truth for Gabriel. I still considered Joelle my closest friend.

"What about you? Anyone you still keep in touch with?" I asked.

"No, I went a little crazy when I found out my wife married my best friend after I was gone," he said, with just a hint of the pain he must have felt.

"Well, you really can't blame her," I said. "She was probably lonely, and you weren't coming back as far as she knew."

That was the pot calling the kettle black. I would be furious if Valderron moved on so soon.

"I know, and I have thought a lot about it," he said. "I *still* think about it. Did it have to be him? He's spending my money and living in the house I paid for. He wasn't the greatest guy. We just had history. He cheated on every girlfriend he ever had. But I'll shut up now because it's not a good subject for me."

We kept cleaning, and I finally switched to my second weapon.

"Strange things happen when someone dies," I said. I hoped this would give him something to think about. I might need him to forgive me for something in the future, and I needed to know he had it in him.

"Do you want to know what I did?" he asked.

"Do you want to tell me?"

"Yes, I do. I thought I was pretty smart at the time," he said.

"Okay, then tell me," I said, and smiled to lighten the mood. He didn't smile back. His intensity peaked.

"I went back home on one of my first real vacations on the job, incognito of course. I hired this guy to take a letter and hide it in a box full of all my personal items that should have come back with my supposed remains," he said and paused, wondering if he should go on with the story.

"Did he actually do it?" I asked, in disbelief. It was more than a little bit funny, and it surpassed what I did with my prank calls.

I didn't feel like such a loser.

"No, because Charles intercepted him and told him I was a terrorist and if the guy didn't cooperate, he would have him sent to Guantanamo or worse," he said, with disgust.

"That's hilarious," I said, thinking about Charles doing that. Gabriel was smiling now too as if he suddenly realized the humor in everything. "What was in the box?"

"Basically, a note saying not to marry my best friend. I guess you're right," he said. "It is kind of funny. Charles didn't think so though. A colossal mistake—his words. At one point I thought he would kill me over it. I think the only thing stopping him was my family connections. And I promised to be a good boy and to go wherever he sent me."

"And you came here?" I said, wondering if this was why he was a liability.

"I wish," he said. "Not at first, I had to earn this assignment in some ways. I started out in Laos, running the most dangerous kinds of operations with little support or backup from Charles or my new handler. He was pissed off, and it showed. Hard work and my good sense prevailed."

"And now, you're here with me?"

"Yes, I am. I feel lucky to have this assignment. We have a

lot of targets on that list, but our living conditions are paradise compared to the holes I've been crashing in."

I took notice of him praising the assignment, not our relationship or whatever it was.

Time flew by as it always did nowadays, and the humidity drew us back to the air-conditioned coolness of the villa.

While Gabriel secured the weapons in a side room, I shuffled through the mail I picked up on the way in. A note from Charles, unsigned of course.

"She's doing well and in love with a very handsome man. His name is Gianni."

That bastard left it at that. The information was not enough. I wanted to know more about Joelle. How did she meet Gianni? Where was she living? Still in Missouri? Who approached who?

Even with all the questions, there was also a sense of contentment. In another life, I thought they would be perfect for one another. I had even told Gianni, my former FBI colleague, about a dream I had where he married Joelle after a particularly long day at work. I showed him tons of photographs of Joelle to hopefully spark something. We both laughed like crazy at the time, but maybe it could work out for them.

At least Joelle might not mope around the same town for the rest of her life. She could go anywhere she wanted, and she had a genuine interest in helping others. I wanted her to explore a bit and get away from the comforts or more like the confinements of home.

Inside the note was an IP address. It looked like an encrypted site. I put the paper in my desk. I would look at it later. Maybe Charles would give me more information.

Gabriel came back from the storage closet.

"You look happy," he said.

"I am," I said, agreeing. "I got a note from Charles about my girlfriend I was telling you about. She met a guy,"

"Oh, that's nice," he said. "Are you going to write her back and tell her you have a partner, someone good for a little slap and tickle?"

The idea of writing Joelle threw me for a loop. I couldn't say a word. That's how it would be for the rest of my life. Could Gabriel contact his parents? It seemed a little unfair, but maybe with their history it made sense for them to know more than the average citizen.

"Maybe once we get through this mission," I said. I was lying about the most basic things, the kinds of things that built a relationship. "I don't want to get her hopes up if one of us takes one in the chest."

"Not funny, honey," he answered, looking all too serious about my little joke.

We went to the beach later that day. It reminded me of home, and the sand was still warm from the setting sun. Nature's splendor surrounded me, and I was grateful for an assignment where the sun still shone, and the water was near. I had to keep my thoughts about my parents at bay.

We rented a hotel on the tourist-filled strip. It was better to be away from all the plans. I had been joking earlier but death was certain, and this job made it a possibility that it would happen sooner rather than later. If I died young, my plastic face would keep me from being identified. I resigned myself to the maintenance required to keep up the lie that the face created.

Before I entered the private plastic surgeon's operating room in Brazil, Charles comforted me by saying that, in a few years, surgeries like mine would be as common as getting your teeth cleaned.

When I took off the bandages, gone were the traces of my parents, my laugh lines, and the wide set nose I once despised. I cut away my old self and began a new one. I had been pretty, cute but not beautiful. I decided cute should have been enough. Why didn't Gabriel have to change his face?

I stretched out on the hotel's white beach chair and gazed up at the horizon. I took in the endless expanse and closed my eyes, breathing deeply.

I was wearing a pair of beige capri pants with a flashy turquoise blouse belted at the waist with a chocolate brown belt. I fit in perfectly with the foreign crowd, not overdressed but still modern and stylish. The hotel made quick work of accommodating us after Gabriel slipped the manager an extra hundred-dollar bill. A wedding made getting a room next to impossible but someone else got bumped and we took a suite facing the ocean. Gabriel wanted to stretch his legs and went for a walk along the beach. It gave me a chance to relax alone, something I didn't realize I might need.

A group of teenage girls were huddled a few chairs down from me. From their accents, I could tell they were local, and I was pretty sure they were with the wedding party. Their conversation had me smiling after just a few seconds of eavesdropping. If this had been pre-Gabriel, I probably would have moved seats or avoided them, but today they didn't bother me.

They seemed to be speaking about the bride, an older sister to one of the girls. I didn't open my eyes, but their voices carried to where I was.

"We should switch the seating arrangements so you and Marcos can sit together," one said.

"No way! He would know I liked him, and he is going to have to work for this," the other responded. Laugh, laugh, giggle, and giggle.

Their laughter was refreshing, and I couldn't remember a time I was that naive. Except for maybe when they were convincing me to risk death and insanity over a prison sentence.

"What if I switched seats to sit next to him and then you come over to talk to me so that it's not so obvious?"

"That's a good idea," one of the girls chimed in.

The girl who liked Marcos replied, "But, what if he checks you out instead of me?"

"Girl, then I won't look back. I wouldn't do that to you. You know I don't like Marcos," she said.

Yeah, right. If I felt like jumping into their conversation, I would have told the girl who liked Marcos that, yes, girls do that sort of thing to each other.

She was smart to consider everyone's motives. Maybe her friend could be trusted but it was during my own teen years when everything went to hell, friends included. My parents died, leaving me alone. Older men were the only ones paying a gullible preteen that kind of attention. I'd cried enough for what happened to me as a teenager the one year I lived with my aunt. The tears could fill the entire Olympic-size swimming pool, and to even water the surrounding palm trees. I slowly began to trust again when my parents' estate was finalized and Jimm and Chantrea stepped in with their new rights and gave me the possibility of a normal life.

My adventurous spirit had been a family joke when I was a girl, but it became a problem when combined with my unstructured home life after my parents' death. How different could things have turned out for the Chapas? I may have cared enough to keep my family name. I may have gotten married. Would I have chosen the military? I didn't know my parents' feelings about everything at all.

I considered the new style of bathing suits one of the older girls wore, a one-piece with the sides cut out. I wanted to try it on. I still considered myself too petite, though I had gone up a size.

"How much Barbie doll do you want to be?" Charles had asked.

"Fake enough to get you off my back about safety, mission success, and anonymity."

And it was just the right amount. These girls were still young and at the peak of physical beauty. But many South American teens and women had some form of plastic surgery, and it was becoming even more accepted back home. I kept repeating this fact to convince myself I fit the new me.

These girls would probably change some part of themselves in the next few years. Joelle and I had endlessly discussed her abhorrence of all things fake, but that was easy for her to say. She looked her best au natural—tall and thin was always in style. I got a second chance at being considered beautiful when Jennifer Lopez started putting insurance on her big ass. Suddenly, it became "in" to have Chapa-style curves. I now looked thinned out, but I kept my butt, and, with a new chest to match, I could rival any actress. Charles hadn't told me before the surgery that, along with all of the body parts, the agency would inject me with even more self-doubt.

At some point, I drifted off to sleep in the chair.

Gabriel whispered in my ear and I came out of my dream.

At least I thought I had been dreaming something. Once he saw me wiggle awake, he asked, "Want to go get something to eat at the hotel? Or do you want to go out, maybe get room service?"

"Hotel is fine, and then we don't have to stink up the hotel room with all your food," I said.

He smiled and said, "I like garlic so sue me. I am half-Asian. You haven't smelled anything until you've sat in my mom's kitchen." He looked past me, returning there in memories. I hadn't been in his mom's kitchen but remembering Chantrea's Cambodian dishes were enough to make me homesick.

The reflection of palm trees in the water made the pool a mirror, which made me want to jump in with all my clothes on and bring him down with me. He was remembering a life he couldn't return to. I was sure.

"Come here, woman, and lay next to me," he said.

He dragged the chair next to him closer. I sat down in the chair.

He didn't say a word but lay on my lap and wrapped his arms around my waist.

His breath warmed my blouse, and I closed my eyes again. This was intimacy in its purest form. Sometimes women forget how tender a man can be.

I heard giggling in my direction, but I just smiled with my eyes closed. Let the ladies look. They were all envious of the man who held me tight, in full view, for everyone to see. What could they say? "Get a room!" Well, we already paid for a room and this pool was part of the deal. We weren't kissing or touching or doing anything in an inappropriate way. I observed beaches all over the world and we were just cuddling, and I wasn't ashamed. I wanted him to do more, but that need was always there around Gabriel.

We lay together until the grumbling in my own stomach woke me up.

Dinner was mussels in a tomato garlic broth as an appetizer, and tiger shrimp and fried calamari for the entrée. It was more than I expected, and the chef knew how to prepare seafood just right.

It made me think of Miami.

Back in our hotel room, Gabriel turned on a soccer game and settled in to watch two local club teams face off.

"I can't believe you like soccer," Gabriel said, after I snuggled up beside him.

"Honey, I'm from here. It's our sport. Every kid in this country has a football and is playing with it as we speak. They will kick anything around, a can, a basketball. It's in our blood," I said. Part of that was true.

Gabriel's phone rang.

"Oh, no, just as the game was getting started. What's going on?" I asked.

"How am I supposed to know?" Gabriel answered.

"Then find out," I said and leaned closer to him to try and hear what Charles relayed to him.

All I heard was Gabriel's side of the conversation, which wasn't much. His face read nothing as well. It couldn't be bad, because surely he would register surprise or panic if it were.

"Uh huh, okay," he said. He hesitated but then confirmed. "Okay. Yes, nooooo, yes. We're on it. Bye," Gabriel said, and hung up on the phone.

"It looks like we have a little more work ahead of us, but the possibility of more money as well."

"Okay, explain," I said, anxious to hear more about the money part.

He lay back on the bed, looking around as if he could see whether the room was bugged or compromised.

"Basically, all you need to know is one of my women just became more of a priority. It seems she was very adept of taking over the family business," he said.

I understood: the William's sister was fully in control of all her sister's operations. Maybe even her late brother in-law's arms deals. We women are a resourceful bunch.

At some point I fell asleep again next to Gabriel. No more phone calls woke us up.

Chapter Nine

JOELLE AND GIANNI WERE RUNNING SIDE BY SIDE ON A LONG gravel road lined with large trees, with a house in the far distance. That had to be her farmhouse, and, to my amazement, where she lived was beautiful. I clicked on the program's magnifying glass to get a closer look.

After a few clicks I could see both, sweating after running only a half a mile away from what I guessed was her house. I hadn't seen it. I remembered a little bit of what Joelle had told me about the Victorian-style farmhouse in Canton, Northeast Missouri, with the trees, colorful and vibrant and the long, winding along the road leading up to her home.

That was the value in having an escape to go to. If I remembered correctly, she didn't live near town, but that was the appeal. I begged her to go in on something together in Miami, where we could live and work together just as we did on deployment. She wanted to live in her own town, and she left the military when I did. Though she never actually said it, I felt she was done following me around, especially after the last deployment, when the body bags were piling up.

She did have a little bit of Miami scenery as well. Gianni was as handsome as ever, and he looked a little out of place jogging next to Joelle, but he was a city boy and I couldn't blame him. She seemed confident and she must have been in her element. He cared enough to fly up and visit her in Corn Country as Joelle had called it. I couldn't save the photo—no evidence of my little spying game could be left around—but as I stared, I tried to cement the image of her being okay without me in her life. I deleted the file and emptied the trashcan on the desktop. Two of my friends had met because of me, so I still had an imprint in their world. This satisfied my ego a bit. A little, little bit.

A day before we separated for our respective missions, Charles called us to the safe house for a little pep talk. At least, I assumed it would be a pep talk, and I wore a flowy white dress, with the base of the knee-grazing bottom dyed as if it had been dipped in a iris-colored paint. It was a fun little purchase from an emerging Argentinian designer. My strapped silver sandals gave me another two inches next to Gabriel. He wore blue jeans and a tight grey tee. We were dressed for a casual outing, but Charles looked all business. His perfectly polished dark brown boots and three-button suit made him look ever the British statesmen.

No cheerio or good afternoon when we came into the apartment. He looked us over with a restrained smile and invited us to be seated.

"So now that you're here, I need to get going," Charles said, looking us over. "It's your target; she seems to be doing your jobs for you. A bit sloppier, but at this moment, Paltrini, your list is down considerably, and Gabriel, you little devil you. You have a real-life praying mantis on your list. She killed her own man, number three on Paltrini's list. We have intelligence they were lovers."

He held up a printed copy of the same list we were given just a short while ago. He tore off all the names, women and men, until one remained—just her. Saditha Sangjani alone remained, and the small strip of paper seemed to symbolize how vicious yet efficient she was. She'd taken out half my list, probably using the muscle I was targeting to do the job, or she could have hired outside, because that was a lot of names. But why? Did she suspect her own people of offing her sister? Saditha Sangjani was just a pup, younger than me at twenty-four years old. What was happening to our generation? Too much violence.

"I know what you are thinking, and I can't answer those questions, but I do have someone who might be of some assistance. He comes from our headquarters in the D.C. area, but has been running our surveillance ops on the Williamses and now Sangjani. Give him your undivided attention because this is all we got. Your job looks like it just got easier, but if you think so, you are dead wrong. In fact, the leadership considered negotiating with Sangjani so maybe we could learn her contacts."

A short, thin man, forgettable in almost every way, came into view. His tanned face was lined with wrinkles and framed with a mess of greasy brown curls. He dressed cheaply, though this could be a cover. He oversaw surveillance, and therefore had to blend in. I wouldn't have noticed him, and I was trained to look for these types. He could have been another piece of patio furniture if I'd seen him at the coffee house downtown or in any public environment. The only way this guy would stand out is in a private, members-only situation. He could crash a wedding at a country club, and someone would hand him an apron and put him straight to work.

I appreciated my disguise, but vanity could be dangerous in my line of work. Alex came and stood over us. As we sat on the couch, I noticed Gabriel had pulled a small notebook from his back pocket, and, after rummaging through my purse for a pen in full view of the other men, he was all set to take notes. He might not have grasped the situation, but a man digging through a woman's purse is extremely intimate. He checked the ink color. He wouldn't want to take any serious information down with a purple, sparkly pen. Gabriel had made that mistake before at a hotel. I liked my colored pens. I appreciated this reminder of my girlhood.

Alex introduced himself, shaking Gabriel's hand and politely bowing to me. I appreciated the gesture. Besides his appearance, he made a nice impression. I responded by nodding my head and giving a slight smile. Alex began speaking with a defiant Baltimore accent. Baltimore natives had their own language. I trained in the area but mostly I learned the pronunciation from watching the HBO series, *The Wire*, one of my favorites when I deployed.

"Well, I've got to tell ya. This woman is more dangerous than both of you put together," he said. I begged to differ, but he was the one familiar with the target. She could have killed puppies or kittens for all I knew. That was a hard limit for me.

Something made me not want him to continue. I didn't like the part where I had to hear what people were capable of doing. I wouldn't want to hear the information if there weren't a payday attached. Offing someone who was more damaged than I was may give me the feeling of a job well done, but some of these people were sick in the head and never had a chance in this world. That realization didn't help to chase away the nightmares when I was taking the garbage out.

Alex continued the briefing and passed out the latest surveillance shots from their detail on Sangjani. They were basically different versions of Sangjani packing up with her personalized staff and yelling at a man newly familiar to me. He was one of my targets, Jose Garzo, a bad apple with a tattoo from his Honduran gang days. Apparently, he fed pieces of his local members to hungry dogs while they were still alive if they crossed him. Somehow, he was one of the few remaining and working for Sangjani. She was handling her own clothes, computer, and paperwork according to a printout of the timeline Alex gave us.

"She's doing all this herself. I thought we were dealing with some elite drug lord of the Pakistani mafia."

"Oh, don't let the looks fool you. She was shrewd enough to be hands-on in her escape. She killed those closest to her sister, as you already heard. Many of them thought she was behind the deaths of her brother-in-law and her own sister. You guys did very well, by the way. There was no way for her to disprove that theory so she killed anyone who she felt could turn against her. That guy, Garzo, is now the only one left who gets anywhere near her in these photos."

"He wasn't around before this?" Gabriel asked. He had been furiously taking notes while I examined the photos. She was originally his target, and he might still do her alone.

"To answer your question, we didn't see much of Garzo before now. He was a go-between, a drug source in Honduras and Nicaragua, but he got a whole hell of a lot more important this past week. Our best guess is she had to look outside for assurances they would get the job done. Garzo himself is not afraid of anyone or any backlash. Sangjani is still reeling from her overseas customers possibly abandoning her for offing her own family. It's just a rumor, but they don't know. She got rid of anyone who perpetuated that theory."

"What are these overseas customers going to do once they are all gone?" I asked.

"That's above my pay grade, Ms. Paltrini, but just guessing, they might take their business to the cartels in Central America. There, we have so many operatives and insiders that we'll get everything on those guys. We'd have 'em by the balls."

Alex's face flashed with wild excitement. He might only be in surveillance, but this was the kind of guy who looked at the bigger picture. He had Washington's best interest at heart, and I liked that intensity. If he just took orders, we might not have the Williamses or Sangjani at this point. His work would hopefully lead to their demise and he was an important link in the chain in South America. Charles sat down in a chair. He seemed too roused by the possibility of having whoever "them" was by the balls. What did I know? We would be the team to bust them.

When any information made it clear that someone was better off dead, that was when I would come in. I had come so far. In Iraq, Joelle used to say, "You can't kill them all." But we damn sure were trying.

"So, what does this mean for the time frame of our mission if she leaves?" I asked.

"Oh, she's gone already. As we speak, she is relaxing in Colombia, getting out of the area and 'mourning' her loss. However, Garzo and a few remaining muscle are still in Argentina. Garzo thinks he's holding down the fort, but he is just a pawn because whether it's the Pakistanis or us, he will be the first to go."

"When are we getting this new intel?" Gabriel asked.

"Right now," Alex said, and handed Gabriel a large folder and me a few pages.

Gabriel didn't seem to notice the discrepancies in our papers. He gave me a side smile.

Before he left, Alex came and patted me on the back. He reeked as if he'd been sweating all day in a garbage truck, and maybe he had. How else did his team get close to men like Garzo?

"Miss Paltrini, I know you don't take any requests, but for Garzo, remember he is nothing less than a cannibalistic dog. I would give anything to acquire your skillset for this one job. If it gets done and you live to tell about it, I will sleep happy after so many nights of seeing his carnage unleashed."

"Well, Mister... your last name escapes me, Alex, I will do this with you on my mind. Keep doing what you're doing."

The guy stunk to high heaven, but it would truly be an honor to take Garzo out for the people like Alex who were always doing the thankless jobs. I knew I made more doing one-tenth of the work he put in. I did have the body counts on my soul, but I'd sort it out later. Maybe my parents could help me do that.

After I made this promise to Alex, I looked over at Gabriel. He wasn't smiling. He looked worried and I knew he wanted to switch with me but Sangjani was just as deadly, and he knew it. She had the money and power behind her and would reap much more of a reward, female or not. Those lines disappeared after we joined the agency. We had to remember women were just as important and were harder to find or mislead. Sangjani wasn't going to be easily manipulated.

I gave Gabriel a look that said, "I'm aware of the danger and capable of handling it."

Alex left us and Charles shook our hands and left. I didn't get a chance to thank him for the information.

"Are you ready to go home?" I asked Gabriel, feeling the weight of the upcoming task.

"You go on, I need to do some shopping," he said, softly.

"Change of plans?" I asked.

"No, mostly a change of tactics and, more importantly, a change of clothes."

I wasn't exactly sure I understood, but I left him alone. He would get a taxi to do his errands. Instead, I went home to sleep, my favorite medication.

Chapter Ten

I LOOKED LIKE A PROSTITUTE IN TOO-TIGHT JEANS AND A HALTER top. I wore my red extensions swept into a messy looking ponytail, used a heavy hand with the eyeliner, and lined my lips like I saw the working girls do.

I took advantage of every remaining flaw I still had and made myself into someone who blended in where Garzo hung out. I dirtied my white flip-flops with mud and stuck trash to the bottom.

I slipped in a fake belly button ring that had a rhinestone cross in the center. It would be my protection when I entered the lion's den. I got a spray tan with my bathing suit to give the impression of being a beach bum or even a dumb ass who got spray tanned in a bathing suit.

After prepping, I looked older than my twenty-eight years, dressed like a teenager. This was my cover, and when I stepped out of the bathroom in all my glory, Gabriel did a double take.

A fake tribal tattoo imprinted on my lower back completed my look. He looked the polar opposite of me, an Asian Rico Suave. He looked sexy. He looked hot. He even unbuttoned the first three buttons of the dress shirt underneath his styled suit. He was good enough to eat. I knew it wasn't for me, but with the look on my face, Gabriel knew I liked what I saw. He lingered for just one second, until he reached around my waist and cupped my ass with both hands.

"I like the look," he said. "Even the tramp stamp."

I could only imagine if it was real. Forever, I would be known in the agency as the tramp stamp killer. It had a nice ring to it.

I felt his fingertips on my lower back, caressing my skin. He inhaled my scent, but he didn't kiss my lips. I had on quite a bit of clown makeup.

This was where the feelings made these jobs more complicated. One of us may not return. He wouldn't have to get intimately close to anyone, but this target might call for something a bit more than the usual job. Killing someone was a bit like sex itself. The stalking, the anticipation, the planning, the rush of pure adrenaline right before the act and the feeling afterwards. My plan for Garzo was up close and personal as well, but I did not want his hands on me at all. I wanted him to be a quickie.

We walked out together. He had a car waiting to take him to the airport and I was driving a rental car.

I stored my various weapons in the larger of my suitcases, which would be delivered to my cover place by another contact, maybe one of Alex's crew, since they seemed to blend in where I was going. I knew Alex wouldn't pull out until the job was complete so for the next couple days, all eyes were on me. Gabriel pulled me close to him.

"You come back, kid," he said. "We got a lot of hard-earned money to spend."

"Same to you, and don't do anything I wouldn't do," I warned, with a finality in my voice.

"Ay, ay, captain," he said, as if we were two buddies going to war. On one hand, we were.

I drove through the city and handed off my suitcase. The rest of the trip would take hours, and I put in a book on CD to make the time go faster. It was *The Alchemist* by Paulo Coelho, one of the most famous novels around the world.

Joelle was a fan, and I picked up the book on compact disc on one of my shopping trips with Gabriel. He seemed surprised and told me it was one of the best books he had ever read.

Joelle had sworn up and down that even though it wasn't necessarily a romance, I would like this book. It was shorter in length than all her other books so I agreed that someday I would read it.

As I drove, the voice of the actor Jeremy Irons almost lulled me to sleep, but then about an hour in, I got very curious about the ending, and I got hooked. Reading a book and driving to work; I was a real multi-tasker. I was proud of myself and decided that after I came back, I might pick up a real paperback book. The last time I read anything for pleasure was the throwaway romance novels my mom left me over ten years ago.

The driving made my thoughts drift and eventually they found their way to my mother. I wondered if she would be proud of me. The retelling of certain stories was important in our family.

"You know what your daughter did, Carlos," she said, as she prepared a dinner.

I was five years old, and I was nervous that I was going to get in even more trouble than I already was at school.

"Tell him what you did, Concepcion," she said, smirking. "To her teacher!"

"I used the scissors..." I said, tentatively.

He nodded, encouraging me, "And what did you do with those scissors?"

"Well, she was bending down to help me untie my shoes and then I just used them to cut her hair, like Mommy does sometimes...."

My mother started laughing. "She cut a chunk out of this lady's afro and it left her sixty-year-old hair-do really messed up. De madre!"

"She did that?" he said. A slight grin.

"Yes, and I pissed her off because I told her she shouldn't get too close to anyone with scissors," she said. "The teacher's the one who put the scissors on her desk. Little kids can't be trusted with those."

I thought of their way of raising me. The versions of acceptability that didn't fit exactly with our Puerto Rican family. I realized as an adult that my parents were not strict disciplinarians. They would humor me. I could argue and debate, but I had to have my facts straight. And I had to be willing to take action if I wanted to prove my point. The memory brought a dull ache of grief as I thought about how much of my life they had missed. And how much of them I missed.

By the time I arrived in Montevideo, there were just a few more minutes of the book left. I considered driving around the city and listening to the rest of the book, but I had work to do.

I switched out cars and arrived a block away from the hideout in a run-down apartment complex. There were something like thirty floors to the building, and I was near the bottom. Floor five—hopefully low enough for a quick exit.

My suitcase was on the bare box spring mattress in the middle of what might serve as a bedroom. I opened the case and examined my options. A sniper rifle in several pieces lay on the first layer. The second layer contained two Beretta nine-millimeter handguns, my signature weapon.

In addition to the guns, I packed various acidic chemicals, for either disfigurement or disposal, depending on the length of time they were used. These were for Alex's benefit. I had several pairs of gloves, and a thinning knapsack to stuff what I could inside.

I would not carry anything with me but the small shoulder bag. Not a handgun. I patrolled the streets, starting around midnight. Garzo would come outside later at night, so that's when I would reveal myself. I walked up and down the decaying block of buildings, staring down at my shoes whenever his goons stared from across the street.

I hunched my shoulders and stuck out my belly a bit. Bad posture was crucial to this disguise. A long brown cigarette dangled from my mouth, and I decided early on I could use the ashes to take someone's eye out.

It was a little game I liked to play; I imagined what could help me out in a fight. A rusty garbage can lid, a puddle of oil in the middle of the street, and my small knapsack. Hell, I could use some of the broken pieces of concrete on the sidewalk if I had to.

The group of men would occasionally look at me, but they didn't detect what I was doing. The worst kind of surveillance was trying to look busy. I looked bored and restless. I could be a prostitute or someone's girl on the side.

I stared with intensity at one of the men guarding the door. He smiled back. I looked away. I had to play it up a bit, so I continued walking and found a stoop out of view to sit on. Taking out a used Nokia cellphone, I played a game for a good thirty minutes. He had to wonder what I was up to. I opened my compact mirror and stared at my reflection, just enough natural beauty to shine through all this makeup and costume. He'd still want me, Mr. Door Guard Number One. He'd help me along.

I came back down the same street with my cellphone on my ear. I kept talking to myself and gave the guy a flirty smile. He pointed me out to his buddies, and they nodded approvingly in my direction. Like clockwork.

I flipped closed my phone and tentatively approached the group of men. "How's the corner, boys?" I asked, breaking through the street noise and the music they were playing with my question. "Any action I should know about?"

I looked up and down the street like I knew I was looking for more than the typical scene on the street.

"It depends on what kind of action you're looking for?" Mr. Door Guard Number One answered. I took a deep breath and glanced inside of the window of the first floor. It looked like a card game was going on inside. I wondered where Garzo was and if he was at the table. So close to me but sheltered by these goons. The three of them took their turns checking out my assets.

"I'm looking for the kind that pays enough to make it out of the hole I'm in," I said, trying to look scared and needy at the same time; nothing like desperation to make a good whore irresistible.

"I might have what you need," Mr. Door Guard Number One said as he groped himself through his jeans. His buddies chimed in. "I got some of that too. Oh yeah, we got plenty for what you need."

"How much for all three?" I asked.

"How much do you need?" one of them asked.

I furrowed my brow as I was trying to calculate an invisible debt.

"Two thousand pesos," I answered.

"You've got to be kidding me," he said. "Too high for something I can get for free."

"Move it along," the other guy said. I was losing them.

"But I need it for rent...my mom will be out on the street," I said, as I envisioned the predicament.

"Like her daughter then," one said, and spit on the ground at my feet.

"I'm not on the street. Some asshole that gave me a tattoo just robbed me. He took everything, including my bill money," I said as I turned around, looking helpless while they examined my bodywork.

One of them whistled.

"I'll give you one thousand if you come back in a half hour when I'm done."

"Fine," I agreed, reluctantly. He'd probably rip me off too if he had the chance. He wouldn't.

I went and sat across the stoop, looking bored. When they weren't looking, I slipped away. I walked back to the apartment and retrieved my Beretta with its silencer. I placed a second weapon, a blade, along the inside of my leg. Either way, I would take them out tonight. I wasn't going to wait until tomorrow.

Sure enough, Mr. Door Guard Number One was waiting for me by the stoop.

"So how old are you?" he said. Why did guys always want to know how old I was? Wasn't a blowjob from a near thirty-year-old just as good as one from an eighteen-year-old? It was all about the ego.

"I'm nineteen," I said.

"I bet you are," he answered.

Once we were out of sight of the street, I told him I brought protection and reached into my bag and gripped my gun.

I pulled it out, removed the safety, and shot him in the head before he had a chance to say another word. I dragged his body further out of view and waited fifteen minutes.

I wiped the blood spatter off my skin with a wet wipe, ruffled my hair, and went back to the door. I asked the one who refused to pay the thousand what he would pay for seconds. He said one hundred and I agreed.

He followed me to the same alley, and I repeated the process. This was like shooting fish in a barrel. The remaining guy was on his cell phone when I arrived, and I flashed some leg. He hadn't noticed that neither of his friends had come back to the stoop.

He kept speaking into the phone as I approached, something about a car stereo. I shot him in the head. No one was around to notice.

I peeked through the window and saw a group of men. The one who looked like Garzo was playing Grand Theft Auto on an Xbox.

I opened the door and put two shots in Garzo's buddies and, just as he turned, one in Garzo's stomach. Almost done.

"Stupid bitch, you shot me," Garzo coughed, holding his guts in.

Garzo was trying to reach his gun but I blew both his knee-caps out. He was heavy but I managed to zip tie his hands and feet. I reached into my backpack and pulled out a small bottle filled with hydrochloric acid.

"This is for Alex. This is for everyone else you killed while he watched. You interrupted his sleep, you bastard," I whispered, as I dripped it slowly over his face.

He struggled under the pain and the blood seeped through his cheesy black suit. I took off the top of the bottle and dumped the remaining acid on his open wounds, then on his face. His flesh began melting off. He was suffering.

I walked back to the door, aimed, and fired into his right eye, which was covered in acid. I didn't wait for anyone else to come down the stairs. I walked out the way I came in.

My mind was racing, and my adrenaline was up. It was the first time I used acid and I was nervous about not wearing gloves. I looked at my hands but was careful not to touch my face. My clothes were covered in blood spatter and bits of bone; other stuff clung to my bare skin. It was a mistake walking around with evidence all over me. It wouldn't have happened in the FBI. I felt gross. But this came with the territory.

I thought about why I did it tonight. I could have waited another day, but sometimes tomorrow never comes. Patience was not my strong suit. I wanted to get back on the road and to be home first to surprise Gabriel.

No doubt he would return shortly after me. Back at the temporary staging apartment, I didn't hear any sirens, but I quickly changed my clothes. I wet a gym towel from the bag and scrubbed myself over a plastic tarp. I wrapped the tarp around the towel and my old clothes. The cleanup crew would pick them up shortly, I hoped. I wrapped the weapon tightly in newspapers and left it sitting near the tarp.

I glanced around; the place was a dump. It smelled like rotting fried food and I guessed the neighbors cooked everything in grease. Once I felt a bit more human, I walked a few more blocks in the opposite direction from the crime scene and found my rental green Peugeot all gassed and ready for me.

After I maneuvered out of the city, I turned on *The Alchemist*. My mouth was dry. I grabbed a bottle of water, opened the cap, and sipped for the next few minutes. So far, so good. I got my cell phone from under the seat, slipped in the SIM card I found in the glove compartment, and punched in a four-digit code to unlock the screen.

No missed calls or messages. By now Charles would know my targets were dead. Alex would no doubt be moving on to a new assignment with a smile on his face. The job was complete, and I hoped Gabriel would come home safely and soon.

Before long, I was lost in the book, trying to figure out what it all meant. It made the trip seem much shorter. I wondered if Mr. Coelho wrote many other books. If so, I resolved to buy them. I arrived in Buenos Aires and switched vehicles out, back to the Black Honda.

After I thoroughly searched the outside of the car for any little surprises, I started it up and was ready for home. My phone rang before I pulled out of the busy shopping center's parking lot. My shoulders tensed up. It was Charles.

"Darling, excellent work. The police are over at the scene now, and it looks like it will be on the 10 a.m. news," he said. "It's okay though because your man has made contact in Playa Koralia."

"Is he done as well?" I asked, though I was pretty sure a call from Charles, and not Gabriel himself, meant he was still in it.

"No, of course not; she is a lot smarter than some horny guys mistaking you for a prostitute."

"Hey, a girl's gotta do what a girl's gotta do," I said, teasing Charles.

"Well, then you won't mind if Gabriel takes his precious time to get her alone with him in a deep dark place."

The inflection in his voice was supposed to get me going. I did mind, a lot. It was more than jealousy; it was territorial, but what did I expect? No, I decided I wouldn't go to a place where I felt territorial about Gabriel. I would enjoy my time alone, shopping, cooking, and even reading some more books. I exhaled the breath I'd been holding since he called.

"Charles, just keep me updated. My fun is over for now. Hey, maybe you can get me some news on Joelle. That photograph you sent me gave me a lot of hope for my buddy," I said.

"I'll see what I can do," he said. "One more thing, your neighbor seems very interested in what's going on over there. Let's just say we're not the only ones who have you under surveillance."

The CIA watching made me feel safe; the neighbor lady peeping made me feel vulnerable. She obviously needed a hobby. Or she was just smarter than she looked and was wondering how we mysteriously took over the Paltrini villa.

"I'll take care of it, somehow," I said, trying to reassure Charles.

"You will buy better curtains or shades. I hope that's what you have in mind," he said, his voice full of concern. "I heard about the acid thing. Don't get too creative."

"Oh, Charles. You always expect the worst," I said. "I am actually very hospitable. I am Miss Congeniality."

"Think about what you just said, Paltrini," he said.

"I'll do that, just for you, good night."

We hung up and I drove the thirty minutes home. The security lights were on, but from the looks of it, no alarms had been set off.

After I parked and secured the perimeter, I dialed my entry code and went into the house. I pulled out my nine-millimeter Beretta, just in case. Being armed put me at ease; I didn't want to get complacent about my own safety.

I changed into some loose-fitting pajamas and plopped down onto the sofa to watch the news. My day's work was the lead story on South American international news. A longhaired beauty updated viewers who'd just tuned in that there were no leads in a drug dealer's massacre. The agency worked fast because the anchorwoman almost seemed cheerful as she detailed the amount of cash, arms, and cocaine that were found at the scene in Uruguay. She segued into a story about how drug laws in Argentina were more readily enforced and, somehow, I felt even better about doing the deed after watching the coverage.

Brava, Paltrini! Saving one city at a time, single-handedly. Nothing about the two previous hits was mentioned. Any links to the Williamses were not yet established or someone who worked with Charles had buried them for good.

I flipped the channels. TV made me homesick, so I rarely watched it on my own.

There was a show about celebrities on, but I didn't recognize anyone, a pretty young blonde flashing on the screen while her life story played in the background. It made me think about being blonde, and I wondered if Gabriel would like a real change. Being without him made my mind run wild with possibilities. He could be dead right now, or worse, being tortured. Though I'd taken out Saditha's so-called allies,

I hadn't really been in danger, not by comparison. Gabriel was at risk now, not me.

I tried to relax, but I kept wriggling on the couch and eventually gave up getting comfortable. I checked my cell phone. No missed calls. I had enough willpower not to call Gabriel, but I needed some reassurance. I redialed Charles. He did not seem happy to hear from me.

"Yes...is everything okay?" he breathlessly whispered into the phone.

"Yes, and no. I'm just worried about him, Charlie, can I call you Charlie?" I said, being playful.

"No, you may not," he said. "And I'm not your nanny. Don't make me separate you permanently. He's working, you are not, end of story. Good night."

He sounded especially aristocratic now, though I'd bet he was mounting some stallion at the moment, and that's why he was being so mean. I contemplated running away but the last time I did that I almost got myself taken out of the game. Maybe permission would be granted.

"Can I go help him?" I asked Charles, before he could hang up.

"Of course not. Well," he said, considering my idea. "Maybe tomorrow night, if he's still not done. But now I'm hanging up on you and I am telling him about this."

"Fine, good night, Charlie," I said.

I heard him let out a noise of disgust. That nickname was a keeper. My nickname came from Joelle and remained funny, Chapastick. I missed having her around to talk to and relive the good times. And even the bad.

I thought about the time we had to train for a nuclear and biological event using full body, standard issue protective gear.

The person who thought up the exercise was clearly male and ensured any female wouldn't be able to relieve herself like the guys were able to do, simply by pulling down their zipper. I spent hours sweating in the suit before my relief came, and it was my battle buddy, Joelle. Every male member had taken advantage of the bushes and could safely keep the suit on without getting caught.

"Remember when you peed in the chemical suit, Chapastick," Joelle said.

Her using my nickname made one of the most embarrassing moments in my Army career hilarious instead of traumatic. The fact that the army hadn't caught on to the bodily functions of all its members wasn't news.

"Yes I do, and I remember you, Joelle McCoy, putting the suit on after I pissed in it so we could complete our mission." And that was the love of two female soldiers, who despite all odds, would put on the urine-filled suit of a friend and wear it for hours. That's family.

I missed her. I thought about the only man I was allowed to miss. Joelle had known Gabriel (as Sebastian Reeves) too. I turned off the TV and carried my phone into the bedroom. I smelled his pillow and hugged it close.

"You better be safe," I said into the darkness of my bedroom.

Chapter Eleven

THE NEXT DAY WENT IMPOSSIBLY SLOWLY. I SCRUBBED THE HOUSE from top to bottom and cleaned four loads of laundry, most of which were curtains and rugs that could use more tender loving care.

I spent hours on the computer reading Joelle's articles from all the way back since we were in the service. She now worked for her hometown paper. I read every word about the school board meetings she covered and the high school plays she reviewed. It wasn't as boring as I thought it would be because Joelle wrote the articles. She highlighted when a heated exchange occurred between two parties. People were living that life, going to meetings, having kids, working their lives away.

I was working mine away differently. I didn't see any articles from the past several months. I guessed she was spending time with her new man. At three-thirty in the afternoon, I baked a coffee cake and decided to bring it to Ms. Mendoza, the nosy neighbor lady.

Charles's threat came to mind. I contemplated putting a little something inside the caramel goodness, to eliminate any future spying. But that would only serve my interest, not my country.

I put on a pair of khaki capris and a silk short-sleeved blouse with ruffles down the front, and matching diamond studs. My hair was in a loose bun. I took a quick glance in the full-length mirror in my bedroom.

Polished yet informal, she couldn't deny me. I appeared harmless and I had cake. If only Chantrea could see me now, as the lady she tried to help raise after the loss of my mother. I was playing the role of a perfectly respectable social butterfly. I walked the few yards to my neighbor's gate, and I pushed the buzzer to the intercom.

"Diga," I heard a voice say. It was Ms. Mendoza with a straight-forward appeal.

"It's your neighbor, Miss Paltrini," I said. "I am surprising you with a quick hello. Will you buzz me in?"

She didn't answer but she buzzed the gate open. I would see her reaction up close and personal. I plastered a smile on my face, deciding to try and be friendly. Anything would be better than being in an empty house waiting and wondering about Gabriel.

I walked up the sidewalk and noticed what lovely roses, lilacs, and honeysuckles she had lining the house. Either the old lady had a gardener, or she had a hell of a green thumb. Jimm and Chantrea had a vegetable garden behind their Miami home, and I remembered watching them work on it for hours while I studied in my room. Their patience and diligence in the garden and with their fruit trees left an impression about the type of people who had adopted me. In their own ways, they gave me a chance at a better adolescence than I could have hoped for, and I allowed doubt about what I deserved to creep in permanently. I barely registered my time with Jimm and Chantrea in my new life. They weren't miracle workers. A lot of damage had already been done. They would be impressed with the radiance of Ms. Mendoza's flowers. A South American display of amber, apricot, and carmine blooms.

This is what I would open the conversation with, the flowers. She was already waiting with the door opened. I smiled, a little too eagerly. She seemed surprised but returned my smile with one that did not touch her eyes.

"Good afternoon, Miss Paltrini."

"Good afternoon, Miss Mendoza," I said. "What a beautiful garden."

I considered every word and spoke with what I considered a perfectly acceptable Argentinian accent. It could have a hint of something else, but I was supposed to be a long lost relative, so I could be from anywhere.

"*Gracias.* I try to always keep something beautiful to look at. The roses are the hardest to grow in this heat. Do you garden?"

"Actually no, but my parents do. They have a vegetable garden that keeps them full on whatever produce is in season."

"Oh, and where do they live?" she asked.

I panicked. No big deal. I hadn't been asked about my parents directly before.

"Cuba," I said. Cuba was a safer bet because politically it pushed the connection with the United States away from the conversation.

"Oh, yes. Cuba is a lovely little island; how did they end up there?" I was trying to process the correct biography on the fly without giving myself away.

"Oh, it's a long story but generally, party connections," I said, struggling to sound relaxed. "They travel extensively year-round."

I thought it rang true, but I kicked myself for not practicing with Gabriel. The lack of questions was chafing at my conscience now that Gabriel was away on a mission. He readily shared my bed but let my backstory stay a general mystery. Unless he thought he already knew the answers. I was a liability for not practicing this more.

My eyebrows closed together, and I forced a grin while I held the cake in the doorway. I paused and looked around, hoping she would ask me in or at least take the cake off my hands. She thankfully got the hint after I shifted my weight a couple times.

"Would you like to come in?" she asked, gesturing.

"Yes, thank you," I answered. I stepped in and closed the door behind me.

"I will take this to the kitchen," she said, grasping the cake from underneath.

The layout of her home was very similar to mine. At least three levels with a winding staircase leading to the second floor.

Her floors were marble, a lasting stylistic choice, but the rest of the halls and crown molding seemed a bit dated. I had to remind myself that they may be what was considered luxury to her thirty or forty years ago. The colors were a bit dark and the floor-length curtains on the windows made the whole house seem too gloomy for an Argentinian villa. The most vivid colors came from her garden and would be a better choice with all the windows opened to let in the fresh air. The size of the house would be a challenge for a mature woman to keep up without help.

"Miss Paltrini, will you join me in the dining room? I'm just dishing up your lovely cake," she said. Her voice broke my focus on my surroundings.

I walked through the sitting room and noticed the same colors also filled this room. No family photos anywhere. The only art on the deep burgundy walls was a portrait of a young woman's face with a red flower in her hair. Could it be a younger Ms. Mendoza? I wasn't sure, but the woman was absolutely mesmerizing. It was the only bright spot in the room.

A large silver candelabrum sat on a weary looking side table. The dust made it seem dingier, almost finished in black. It smelled like an old man, or woman in this case. The same smell I remembered from twenty years ago at my grandmother's nursing home in Panama City. Musky yet medicinal. The dining room was a bit more updated. The large windows let the light into the room. I guessed Ms. Mendoza used this room for entertaining. The table could seat eight or maybe even ten people. Ms. Mendoza put two pieces of the coffee cake at the end of the table.

"Would you like some coffee or tea with your cake?" she asked.

"Coffee would be great, but I don't want to be any trouble."

"No, it's no trouble at all. I was hoping you would stop by sometime. I bought some fresh cream from the market this morning," she said. I saw a slight smile on her face as she set about making the coffee.

"I'm not used to living in an area where everyone is so friendly," I said, truthfully.

"Oh, we're not friendly all the time but we were curious about the new tenants," she said. "The word is that you were related to the previous owners. Did I get that right?"

She seemed to speak more in her own home, with the comfort and assurance of her things. It took gusto to show up on someone's doorstep. This was the first time in a long time I was putting myself out there to be welcoming.

"I am the niece to Miss Paltrini," I said. "Or I *was* her niece before she died."

"Oh, is that so?" she said. "Did you know her well?"

"No, sadly not, but she left the house to my parents and they wanted me to have a place to call home. That's how I ended up here. Their move to Cuba was fairly recent."

"Oh, I see," she answered. I thought she was buying it.

She took a nice sized bite of my brown sugar swirled coffee cake. It was good. I could tell she enjoyed it. I waited until she finished preparing the coffee Argentine style in the "*cafetera*," a metal coffee pot where boiling water was poured over a cloth and wire filter. After a few sips of the roasted ambrosia, I ate the whole piece of cake in just a few bites. The perfect combination of two handmade and specific tastes. She served us both another piece of cake and then, later, she made me another cup of her coffee. My fingertips tapped the table with energy as we spoke.

"This coffee is something special and even a little sweet," I said. "I've seen coffee made a few times in this way, but my parents preferred espresso."

She gave me a real toothy smile and I could see the fading bits of her dental work. "The secret is that there is sugar in the coffee grounds. No need to add it."

I winked with the knowledge of her hidden sugar placement. She giggled, a much younger laugh that endeared her to me.

She spoke about her parents a bit, and I assumed she never married, but I didn't ask why. At her age, she was probably tired of telling that story. I guessed that she was in her late sixties to early seventies. I carefully commented on her home, trying to give her something she could take away from our visit, casual compliments, and a little laughter.

In the hour I stayed at Ms. Mendoza's house, I learned a lot more than I expected about my nosy neighbor. She had lived here her entire life except for a few years she spent studying at the university. She had three siblings, but she stayed to take care of her ailing parents and everyone agreed she should remain in the house after they passed.

I allowed her to dominate the conversation and found myself enjoying her company. I could end up like Ms. Mendoza for all I knew. The CIA retirement package was rarely discussed with the resident assassins. Could I come back and live next to Ms. Mendoza? I had enough money to buy something nicer but here was as good as anywhere. It would never be Miami, but it was something.

These were questions I did not consider until I was having a conversation with a normal person, even if my own stories were bogus. Yes, she was nosy, but if I had been a proper neighbor and introduced myself to her when I moved in, I doubted we would have caught her searching me out.

I didn't mention Gabriel to Ms. Mendoza because I didn't want to make her uncomfortable. I thought that mentioning a live-in boyfriend who comes and goes might not be proper etiquette for a first-time meeting.

She had met him when she dropped off the package, but why should I give her any information she could use to gossip? I guessed she knew the rest of the neighborhood. Possibly, by using the same methods she used on me. Towards the end of our visit, I worked up the nerve to ask her about the portrait in the living room.

"I noticed the painting when I came through. Is that you?" I asked, plunging ahead with my curiosity.

She smiled, and I could see the years fade away as she glowed.

"Yes, that is me. In my younger days," she said. "*Much younger...*"

"Where was it painted?"

"It was painted by a local street artist," she said. "He signed his name on the back but it's illegible. I had it done with the winnings of my first ballroom dancing competition. He was very good. He passed away shortly after he painted it. Killed by the Perón government."

I nodded. I was sad I made her remember something horrible. I wanted to change the subject from political killings.

"You were a dancer?"

"Oh yes, I still am. I go to the city clubs with a few other ladies every weekend and we dance with what few gentlemen show up. I used to teach dance you know," she said. "Latin ballroom was a favorite of mine to watch as a young girl. The paso doble is the rhythm of our country. It is a man's dance but as you can see, I am not a traditional woman."

She was right. Ms. Mendoza was more like me than I realized. She was playing in a man's world. Going to a dance class sounded almost normal.

"I would like to go with you sometime to have you teach me," I said.

"Really?" she asked. "Well, just come by on a Saturday morning around ten a.m. and you can ride up with us to my old studio. I rent it out currently, but I still have access when there isn't a class going on. You may bring anyone else you like as well."

She gave me a knowing look. I guessed she had just invited Gabriel too.

I left her close to six p.m., and her company put me in a better mood and, more importantly, kept my mind off Gabriel for a few hours. I practically skipped home with empty hands. Leaving her with my cake pan ensured more visits to come and the lonely woman next door suddenly had the makings of a good friend, maybe even a teacher. I loved to dance but I never took the time to focus on learning all the steps. I could salsa like everyone else in my family, but I wanted to know more about the cumbia, paso doble, the cha, the merengue, and the tango.

Once I entered my home, I remembered, and the sickening feeling returned. No calls, no messages, and no emails. With so many ways to communicate, I thought maybe Gabriel could have sent something to let me know how everything ended up.

We had only been apart two days, but I was having the worst feeling. I couldn't imagine what the spouses of soldiers had to endure while their loved ones were deployed. I wasn't used to being the one who was waiting for someone. I liked to be in control of my own happiness.

It was what first attracted me to Chuey Valderron and Gabriel. They both understood at least minimally what my work was about. Once my job moved on from what Valderron and I were doing together, the secrets just became too many to reconcile any new life.

I had to admit I was more than guilty for Valderron's heartache because we really had something good. Gabriel was like a different version of my former fiancé. He was in the same line of work as me, so whatever else happened outside the job felt more complete, even as we shared the typical relationship criteria, like intimacy, too. It was us versus them. I needed to be on the same team as whomever I dated.

To stop obsessing about the past. I started packing a small bag. I would concentrate on doing something other than worrying. I packed my toothbrush, a few miniature versions of my hair products, and a couple changes of clothes. In addition to the more mundane items, I packed a clean Beretta. I didn't know what to expect, but if I forgot anything, I could just buy another one.

I loaded the car and called Charles. I waited until the last possible second to do so. I was ready to go to Playa Koralia whether I had permission or not.

"Hello," Charles answered. "My little rose blossom, where do you think you are going?"

"Well, you apparently already know so why don't you just give me some specifics. Heard any word from him?"

"No but meet me at the apartment in one hour and I will give you my intel," he said.

"You're going to try and stop me, aren't you?" I said, I didn't trust him to just let me go so easily.

"I will not stop you. I promise," he said. I wasn't so sure, but I needed more information if I wanted to see Gabriel without ruining the entire operation.

"I'm taking you at your word, and we both know what that means to you," I said.

We hung up and I sped over to the bookstore in town. I bought another book from Paolo Coelho and a brand-new portable CD player. The old-fashioned way. I would be taking a plane because the trip to Colombia would take days any other way.

I could take the red-eye out of Buenos Aires to Bogota and be in the vicinity of Playa Koralia in another two hours. I got to the apartment only a few minutes before our scheduled meeting.

I let myself in, but Charles was not inside. He arrived a few minutes later as I was taking the wrapping off my newest purchases. Wrappers on CDs were invented by NASA in order to prevent anyone from hearing the contents unless they owned a pair of scissors to scratch it off.

He had another man with him, a very handsome man, and they both looked dressed for a night on the town. Was Charles losing his touch? I nodded to his friend, but Charles made no signs he wanted to speak with me in private. He handed me a file and simply said, "Good luck."

"I'll see you when I get back," I said, trying to reassure him that I planned on returning.

"Fine with me." He was not happy with this venture. But despite his objections, they left me to it.

I spent the next few minutes familiarizing myself with the contents. First, there were photos of Gabriel at a hotel bar chatting with Saditha. He looked great. A few more photos were taken a few hours later. Same hotel but now they were seated at a two-person table. Saditha looked like a Hollywood film star instead of a dangerous drug dealer. So much glamour, even more beautiful than this version of me.

"Well, isn't this cute?" I said, aloud.

My cheeks grew hot and my blood boiled inside my veins. It was no wonder Charles left so quickly. How could he explain this tactic Gabriel was using? I was no saint. I would have preferred the one shot, one kill approach, especially with a young, attractive target.

Gabriel's file included his room number, 302, and a balcony right on the beach. Saditha's room was all the way at the top in the penthouse suite. She was staying there; all that hard-earned money was probably burning a hole in her pocket.

She was only a paycheck to me. I needed an explanation from Gabriel. What was all the fuss about? I recalled his file on her was a lot thicker than mine and I had a gang of vatos. Gabriel had one name, one woman. Maybe her death could spark something overseas with the Pakistani mafia if not staged properly. Charles didn't stop to explain, but everything was on his terms. It was the problem with getting involved with someone you worked with; it was why the CIA wouldn't punish you. Because the job had its own fucked up way of screwing you.

Chapter Twelve

THE FLIGHT LASTED ONLY AN HOUR AND A HALF, AND THE CAR trip from the airport put me in Playa Koralia at six in the morning. As the sun came up, I finished my second cup of coffee and checked in to the hotel under my favorite alias, Chiquita Conseulos.

I wanted to understand my surroundings before I tried to see Gabriel in person. This was very unorthodox, and Charles had warned me multiple times not to go. I surveyed the hotel bar area where uniformed waiters were serving breakfast. Could Gabriel be sleeping off a long night of partying, or was he up in his room preparing for the job? I guessed it was the latter.

He wasn't on vacation. He wasn't relaxing with me. I told myself he wasn't enjoying it, but I had enjoyed some of the jobs I had been on. My first official hit had been off the coast of Brazil, and the island where I stayed had to be a natural wonder of the world. It was early on in the mindfucking, so I still believed my parents would pop out of the shadows and end the charade that a special team or the CIA needed me. I spent my time there trying to make it easy for them and just did what I was supposed to do. They never showed. I was sure they never would.

Besides my own personal drama, Latin America had two things that kept me busy: beautiful beaches and plenty of targets. I checked into my room, 507, two floors above Gabriel, and after surveying the area, unpacked my toiletries and took a hot shower. The water mixed with my lavender body gel burned my spine and lower back with just the right amount of pressure and heat. I needed to unbundle my nerves and used the shower head to release the tension that built around my shoulders and lats. I practiced breathing and slowing down my racing thoughts by imagining I was here for this shower and this moment. I'd made it to Colombia without changing my mind. I made the right decision by coming to help Gabriel. My affirmations made me sure he would think so too.

It was at least ninety degrees outside, and I was trekking through Tayrona National Park at three in the afternoon. Many well-paid tips led me to the area where I thought I should be able to find my partner and his target.

As I walked the path and hiked upward, I kept telling myself that this was a very smart move on Gabriel's part. On the other hand, the hotel staff had seen them leave together. If I could pay for the information, then so could the police. I slogged a couple miles, but it took almost an hour to go up the side of a hill. The hotel concierge had given me a brochure for the area and some of the key spots I might care to visit. The happy couple had left together at around one p.m.

I considered what weapon Gabriel would pack in his picnic basket, or whether he would just drop her off on one of the many sloping cliffs. I was ruining my nails and sweating through my shirt. I wanted to rip out my blonde extensions. I could take any kind of heat, but I hadn't packed properly for a hike through the jungle. I had a light bag for a night in a luxury hotel.

How could I have known Gabriel would bring her up here? He certainly hadn't called or texted me a word about how he was doing. It upset me that after our time together, he would run off and not let me know something. I was weakening where it concerned Gabriel. That was worse.

I finally spotted a group of guests hiking together with a hotel guide. I assumed he worked for the hotel because while he was wearing a polo shirt and khaki pants. Gabriel and Saditha, along with the rest of a hiking group, were clad in practically nothing. I didn't plan for those people.

She had on a pair of mini board shorts and a bikini and Gabriel wore a wife-beater shirt and a longer pair of shorts. He was glistening, in every sense of the word, but I saw no disguise whatsoever. Had he suddenly switched tactics, disregarding everything I was trained to do? I'd experienced loss and indescribable pain by changing my whole appearance, and for what?

I was careful to stay about a hundred feet back from the group, and, the way they trampled along the path, no one seemed to notice me lurking behind. No, this wasn't on me. It was on Gabriel.

When the group stopped for a rest, I did too. I checked my cell phone for any messages from Charles or even Gabriel just in case he'd decided to update me. Nada! I heard voices approaching but stayed crouched behind a tree in my strappy sandals.

I had lost five pounds of pure sweat, but I'd prepared by hydrating plenty the day before. I would make it. The temperature was nothing, but the humidity was giving me problems. Now, as the group turned back and I was digging like an animal in the jungle, all the creepy crawlies making friends with my bare legs, I started regretting my decision to come here. I heard the group pass but when I peeked through the trees, I saw that Gabriel and Saditha were not with them.

They were hanging back on the path. What were they waiting for? The next time I dared to look up I was sorry I had. Gabriel was kissing her with as much passion as he had kissed me. She wrapped her arms around his neck, but this didn't look like any awkward first kiss. They had done this before. I was just the poor sucker who was witnessing it for the first time.

I closed my eyes. Tears welled up but I held them back with all I had. No way! Was I crying for this asshole?

When I tried to change positions to leave, I dropped my head down. My hands were balled up in tiny fists. I felt anger instead of sadness. This was good. I could use anger. I pulled my knapsack close to my chest.

I listened to them smacking their lips together. All the sounds I could imagine I was hearing.

I glanced up, and at first I thought they were gone. Then I saw the two lying in the brush surrounded by trees. She was moaning. I crawled low and stopped to apply the silencer to my weapon. I didn't want the group ahead to hear a thing. Or turn around at all. I couldn't off a whole group of tourists.

No, I knew I couldn't. But these two, I knew they were as good as dead. Gabriel was a liability to me, and I could end it any place, any time. Hell, I could even stage it as a murder/suicide. That would mean Charles might have to bring in cleanup, because Gabriel's appearance two years and miles away from Iraq would be more than suspicious. I kept going. He didn't look up as he sat on her body. I couldn't see everything clearly. Instinct told me to kill him first, but I wanted him to know I knew he was fucking a target he could have just killed a million times by now.

Once I checked for any other movement, I crossed the path. I removed my shoes and discarded them along the way. I had the element of surprise and had to keep moving. When I was close enough to reach out and touch Gabriel, I pulled his glistening shoulder off Saditha. Time stood still but I didn't. Our eyes met. Her pupils were dilated with pleasure. I squeezed the trigger and the blast pulled my shoulder back slightly. Half of her head was missing. I fired again into her chest.

Gabriel grabbed me by my legs and pulled me onto the ground. I felt Saditha's body beneath mine and I struggled to get free of him. My throat closed up. I kneed his crotch. He was still dressed. Maybe he hadn't been fucking her but at this point, I didn't care. He released me and was trying to grab my waist as I stood up. He had my gun in his opposite hand. He had control but I didn't hesitate. I bolted, grabbed my sandals off the path along with my bag.

"Wait, it's not what you think. STOP! Don't run off. She was already half-gone. I gave her something." His words didn't register, nothing made sense. If he poisoned her then why was he kissing her? I didn't turn around because I couldn't face him. There was a thin line between love and hate, and I didn't know what would win over if I stayed. I had to get out of the park, away from him. My feet were bloody from the rocks, but I kept running. I didn't feel a thing except adrenaline. I had been running my whole life and this wasn't any different. I trusted him and I was so stupid for him, for my parents, for Aquila. I was living a life I didn't believe in.

I made excellent time, running ahead instead of creeping as before. The park was alive and calling out to me, but I didn't see any of it.

I stopped closer to the entrance by a small waterfall. I was dirty, disgusting. It wasn't all my own blood—it was risky—but I wanted to feel the cool water on my skin. I crouched under a rock and dipped my toes inside. If there was pain, I didn't feel it. I watched the water turn a pinky hue until the cold numbed the cuts and the blood stopped flowing.

I splashed water on my face and neck. Blood was spattered on my blouse, but unless someone was looking for it, I hoped they wouldn't notice. I dialed Charles's cell number and hoped he would pick up right away. I needed instructions. Help. He didn't answer so I texted him a 9-1-1message. He could be on the phone with Gabriel for all I knew.

I tried to smooth the wrinkles from my clothes but there was only so much I could do. I couldn't go back to the hotel and let them connect this to me. I still had a few things in my room, but Charles would have to take care of it. Hell, he might even have Gabriel clean up after me. It was not a good time to get sloppy, but I would just count on his understanding. I completed his assignment, didn't I? There weren't any witnesses there except for the agent who was sent there to do the job.

I walked until I found a bus going to a different hotel. I told the driver I was from an earlier group, and when a group of nubile teenage girls and boys climbed in beside me, the driver had enough passengers to return us to Playa Koralia. They were too engrossed in each other to pay me any mind. They were Colombians, based on their speech, probably on a weekend trip. But I wasn't thinking about them. I was still seeing red, and if anyone so much as touched my shoulder, I might have exploded right there.

We came to a stop in front of another beach side resort. I still had my identification in my knapsack, so I pulled out another alias and checked in as Monica Bunchen. I still had another two available after Chiquita and Monica. Though I wasn't dressed for a hike, I had the sense enough to pack my wallet.

My hotel room was small compared to those in Saditha's hotel of choice, but it was clean and simple now, a refuge from the day's events. I took a shower and removed all my hair extensions. I was lighter. How much had changed since my last washing only hours before. The limited security of my place and my world had faded. My legs were rubbery and bruised and the only thing I comparable to my level of fatigue was the feeling of having run a marathon. I was always screwing up any version of happiness the world gave me. Why, why, why?

I couldn't ask Charles or anyone for an explanation because the weakness I developed over Gabriel would be a game-changer. The agency would deem me unfit, but I couldn't return home after so much work to kill me off. I watched the water from my shower form a pool and circle into the grates of the drain; it ran clean, but I imagined blood and tiny cells of human DNA running into the pipes.

I washed my skin, harder, rougher, and then emerged from the shower. The mirror revealed pink, red blotches where I'd irritated my skin. I needed to feel clean. I didn't dare put any of the mini hotel scented lotions on the blotches. It would only make it worse.

The steam followed me out and fogged up my reflection. I wanted to cry but couldn't. I had to regain my bearings. All the maybes and what ifs raced through my head and I had no hope of finding out the answers. Answers would only complicate. I needed to eat something and rest.

Those two basic needs were what spurred me to action. I put on a short bathrobe made from disposable fibers. At least I didn't have to wear my soiled clothes. I called for room service and ordered steak and seasonal vegetables and coke with a straw. I'd checked my cell phone a few times. No Charles. He must have been busy not to call me back.

I turned on the television to drown out the voices in my head, the same voices that plagued me as my former self, and once again as Paltrini. Time seemed to fast-forward while I zoned out to a Colombian version of *Who Wants to Be a Millionaire*.

The difference in this game was that South Americans were much more attractive than their Northern cousins. Every facet of diversity was covered. In this version of the show, the questions were not as difficult, but the contestants seemed livelier, happier and sexier.

Despite their appearances, class disparity appeared more devastating on this side of the equator. There was no middle class, and it showed. I hadn't visited Colombia as much as other agents. I couldn't understand why Gabriel and I were sent here, or why we were being used instead of the many local CIA agents. Too risky for them. Maybe too risky for me as well. My cell phone rang.

"Speak of the devil," I muttered under my breath.

"Charles," I said into the phone, no need for preliminaries.

"Agent Paltrini! Tell me your side of the story and leave nothing out," Charles said. He'd already spoken with Gabriel. Who was his real priority? Well, Gabriel had the most explaining to do in my opinion.

"I'll tell you everything, Charles, but I just want to say, I am safe and sound for the moment," I said, trying to lighten the mood. "Does that count for something?"

"We'll see, but it's no surprise you can take care of yourself, my dear," he answered. Charles seemed calmer now. Maybe my safety was of value to him.

"First of all, I killed Sad..." I stopped myself mid-sentence. No names. I began telling Charles the story with the most important details first. "With no help from my partner. I found him with the target on the side of a Colombian rainforest trail. Afterwards, there was a bit of a disagreement over who should carry my personal weapon and, with brute force alone, I was disarmed. So, I decided to walk back to safety. He wasn't in his right mind. I came to the location I texted you and now I am awaiting clean clothes, a pile of cash, and my personal weapon. Oh, and I require no more contact with him."

I was pissed and I sounded like a jealous lover, but I wasn't crying my eyes out, so I considered this an improvement.

"So now you are telling me how to do my job? Do I have that right?" Charles said, his voice dripping in sarcasm.

"Sometimes I think it's better to let your leaders know how you want to be led," I said. "I need to be taken care of. After all, I am only doing my job."

"Agent Paltrini, I'm not going to waste my breath and lecture you, but I have to say you were not doing your job," he said. "You were getting personally involved with another agent and using whatever means necessary to fuck up your chance at happiness in and outside of this job. I have to say, I let you go to Colombia because you earned my trust these past few missions. I consider this a failure."

Charles tried to continue but I cut him off.

"I thought you weren't going to lecture me, Charles."

"I didn't, I just told you the truth," he answered. "If I was lecturing you, you would know it. I know better than to argue with a bitch in heat."

Heat? He had some nerve pulling the female card.

"This bitch in heat got the job done," I said, with finality. "Here's a question for you. Why am I here? Where are my parents? When do I join the real team you all forced me into? Why is my face cut up like some real housewives clown and I'm not even thirty years old? Why am I not rotting in a military prison?"

"By my count, that's five questions, not one," he said. "I'll let you calm down after your royal fuckery."

Charles tempered his tone and assured me an agent would be by with everything I needed, but he didn't answer any of my questions.

"You know you drive me to drink, woman," he said. "You will get what you need if I have to bring it to you myself."

A few minutes after I hung up the phone, room service knocked with my steak dinner. I was so hungry that I'd lost my appetite. This usually happened on particularly long missions. I looked out on the balcony, the visceral luxury, and beaches with watercolor skies that surrounded me. All this beauty, and yet so many people who didn't know when they would eat again.

A group considered terrorists, the FARC, operated hundreds of miles away, but from what I read in an article in *Vanity Fair*, the Colombians living under FARC territory had their own system of bartering and were not confined to poverty. The existence of groups like FARC, which successfully took care of large groups of people, mostly with illegals funds, challenged the idea of what a terrorist was.

Anti-U.S. sentiment was very prevalent in Colombia, and many other South American nations. Being of Argentinian parentage, according to my new identity, had many advantages. The longer I stayed on this continent, the more I cared for things like the origins of my identity. Joelle and her ideas were still with me all the way over here.

I ate my dinner with the background noise of the television. The millionaire show was no longer playing, but another game show that featured a greasy-haired host and group of leggy models. I heard a knock at the door again. I looked through the peephole. This guy could also be from the hotel.

I asked instead, "Who is it?"

"Raul Castro, I have some of what you need," the man said.

Raul Castro? This guy was quick with the jokes. Agency. I opened the door for the short young man who resembled the previous bellboy. The real difference was I could see a hint of disguise, but then again, I was looking for the cracks in this guy's facade. It had to be the placement of his words. It was Colombian of course but more textbook Spanish. That's probably why he was an errand boy.

I tied the robe as best as I could, and Mr. Castro entered rather forcefully. He eyed me up and down. Well, he had the attitude and demeanor of a typical Colombian asshole like those I'd encountered at the airport. As if I was a roasting pig on the spit. He sat the bag down and started looking around my accommodations. Who did he think he was?

"Excuse me, Raul Castro, thank you but that will be all," I said and feigned a smiled.

"I have strict orders to make sure you have whatever you need, mami."

"Let me check the provisions and then you can leave," I said, ignoring his salacious gaze. "It's getting late. I want to get some sleep."

"Oh, I will be staying with you tonight," he said, sounding a little too enthusiastic about it. "This hotel isn't sanctioned. The owners are on our Do Not Frequent list."

"Well, how the fuck should I know that? It's just for one night," I said, flatly.

"I understand but we can't have you unaccompanied in this hotel," he said, as he looked around at what he thought he would be protecting. I rifled through the backpack: a deep purple velour track suit, tank top, thirty-four C bra, white underwear, a couple thousand dollars' worth of various currencies (more authentic if I was a traveler), toothbrush, and toothpaste.

It looked like he hit up a few stores on my behalf. I had what I needed, but he couldn't have been serious about staying with me.

"Thank you, Raul, but I will not be requiring any security."

"Oh, yes you will," he said forcefully as he sat near me on the bed. The nonexistent hair on my forearms stood on end. Unsettling and caustic vibes. This guy was a creep. What type of operation did the agency run around here?

"Excuse me, you do not understand, but exactly who do you think I am?" I said, trying to give him the benefit of the doubt. I was slightly embarrassed by using the "who do you think I am" line, but I wanted an answer.

"I didn't get a name, just a room number, but I know you work as an analyst for our Argentinian office, and you came here following up with someone else from the same department."

Before I answered him, I stood up, blocking any exit he might try to make in haste.

"Like typical assholes, a little lie makes it easier for them to get you to come here," I said. "I actually don't work as an analyst, I do something else for the agency, something a little more fun."

He leaned forward. I opened my bathrobe, flashing him my tanned, nude body.

"Te gusta?"

"Sí."

I carried a serrated knife on the side of my hip inside my bathrobe.

My fingers played over the edges of the blade and then the leather handle. Pulling it out would take a few seconds. I pushed him back on the bed.

His body collapsed back, and his arms dropped to his sides. He was stuttering, trying to form coherent words. This little pervert thought he would be sharing my bed.

"Want to guess what it is I actually do?" I asked, in my raciest tone. "I have a few tricks I could show you. A few keystrokes that always stop the guys from looking at me the way you did, Mr. Castro."

My guest tried to find the words and failed—either because of my nakedness or from the knowledge he wouldn't be fucking an analyst to whom he was sent to deliver supplies. I kept my finger on the handle of the blade.

The smartest thing he did was hop off the bed and leave my room. He scurried like a little squirrel. But squirrels were cuter; Castro looked more like a beady-eyed weasel. It wasn't his fault that he was incapable, but he was, most guys were. I needed no more proof.

I locked the door from the inside. What was not inside the backpack was my weapon, lucky for him. I would have to retrieve it later. I dressed, brushed my teeth, and braided my hair into an attractive rope across the back of my head.

Charles had left a number for a cab company, and I dialed

on my cell phone. Once I heard the standard greeting, I gave the operator my location and said, "Airport please." I wasn't sticking around for Raul to find his friends and ambush me. My work here was done.

Chapter Thirteen

THE NEXT FEW DAYS AT THE VILLA PASSED WITH RELATIVE EASE. I disinfected the house of all reminders of Gabriel and had his things delivered to his new location. It was the safe house where he had assaulted me in the bathroom.

Charles delivered my service weapon to my home while I was out shopping. He left it on the kitchen counter with a note about some possible vacation spots if I was so inclined to get out of town. I received both fees for all the targets. No one had proved to be any more dangerous than I was when my reputation was on the line. I wanted to plan something else, but my mind couldn't comprehend what could be next.

I didn't feel like traveling in the immediate future, so I explored the city. I finally found out what my favorite tree was called. La tipa reminded me of the winding weeping willows but more bulbous. I asked my guide at the Botanical Gardens in the Plaza Italia, which had over 5,000 species ,why it seemed like La tipa was crying.

"Is it a sap or something?"

"No, it's actually insects shitting in the tree, and then it falls all over tourists. It's the funniest thing when it happens."

I laughed shyly. I had insect shit all over my favorite blazer. I still loved the tree and I loved knowing that I wasn't considered a tourist by the guide. I needed my inside knowledge.

Spending my time alone at the villa, feelings about the incident flooded back. How could I be so completely...I couldn't think of the right word. I fell asleep on the beach. I awoke with the same thoughts. The world was damaged. How was I so destroyed?

For most of my life, I had a small appetite, except when I prepared some of my mom's favorite recipes. My mom, who was still separated from me by choice. Her choice. Now, I was ravenous, hungry and thirsty. I left the beach and went to the marketplace.

I wanted to drown myself in something, and from previous experiences I knew I would drink, or call Gabriel or Valderron or even Joelle. Drunk dialing at my age and in my occupation was not appropriate, even if they probably deserved to hear what I would say. Because I knew I shouldn't drink, I wanted to eat instead. I was completely aware of how classically pathetic I was, but I wasn't scared of embracing a "cliché."

I baked up a storm in my spotless kitchen. I created different ways of making several messes at once. Pots with red chili sauce bubbled on top of the stove. The oven held fresh bread and the counter was covered in other specialties awaiting their turn in the fire.

Amid a cleaning frenzy, I decided to invite Ms. Mendoza over for a first-class dinner. Who else could commemorate with me? I dialed the number on the l yellow sticky I'd attached near the phone.

"Will it be just us, dear?" she asked, probing for information on my former housemate.

"It is just me and you don't need to bring anything," I said into the receiver. "I have everything we need."

"I'll be over shortly," she agreed. I cleared all the crazy out of her view, though I did see the absurdity of serving her marinated grilled steaks with salted, stuffed tiger prawns, a large pan of paella, two different salads, one corn and one tomato based, and three different desserts, a white coconut cake drenched in sweetened condensed milk, powdered sugar donuts, and a caramel de leche cheesecake, with two loaves of freshly made semolina bread.

Just as I finished setting the table for two, I heard the doorbell. I answered the door in a pair of jeans and a tank top. I hadn't had my long-awaited bath yet. I was going to save it for later.

Ms. Mendoza arrived with a vase in hand with a vivid arrangement of colors from her garden. I especially loved the stargazer lilies and the roses, but there was the garnish of cockspur corals that stole the show. The five fiery and flaming petals of Argentina's national flower reminded me of the folklore surrounding its namesake. In my research of my new home, floral considerations were thankfully included. A young indigenous woman, Anahi' was tied to a tree and burned alive after killing her Spanish captor. When her killers returned for her body, the flowers were blooming instead.

"Thank you for coming," I greeted her, and took the vase, remembering the story.

"Oh, thank you for inviting me," she said.

"These are lovely," I answered. "I will put them as our centerpiece. I love the cockspur corals."

"I am happy to bring them to one of my new friends," she said, as she looked around the entrance area of the villa. "You have a very interesting esthetic."

It wasn't her taste, but everything was from the latest home design stores in Argentina. I appreciated her comment though. She wasn't faking that she liked it, the way I did with her home. None of those things mattered in the end.

"Come into the kitchen to see what I made for dinner," I said.

Once in the kitchen, I watched her expression as she looked over the food. She seemed pleased as she eyed the spread. She needed to taste it before she made up her mind.

"It looks delicious," she said. "Let me wash my hands and we can put all of your hard work on the table."

I showed her the bathroom and left her to finish bringing in the dishes to the dining room. She could have washed her hands at the kitchen sink, but that was too familiar. She probably wanted to look through my bathroom cabinets. I might have done the same thing.

A few bites into the steak she remarked that it needed something else.

"The red sauce, I left it to keep warm in the oven," I said.

When I placed it in front of my guest, she did as I would have and dumped the sauce over her steak. Before she took a bite, she stuck her pointer finger into the sauce and tasted it. I hadn't made the sauce for at least a couple years now; I had last made it for Valderron, as I recalled.

"It's a bit spicy for my taste, but very well balanced with the heat," she said, as if delivering an important verdict. "This is not something we would have in Argentina. I like it. But some time we need to have an asado, with all my friends. You don't have any you want to invite?"

Whatever she thought about the food, she ate like it was her last meal. When was the last time this amount of food was placed in front of the aging dancer? I couldn't have predicted it when I bought out the whole marketplace, but together we put away a couple steaks, all the shrimps, most of the salads and half a loaf apiece. A chorus of gluttony.

I could feel my jeans cutting into my too full, but satisfied belly. It was Thanksgiving dinner down South. I honestly couldn't comprehend eating dessert. We took a break and I brought out some bicarbonate version of Alka seltzer for the predicted side effects of two ladies unaccustomed to gorging themselves on spicy food. I hoped the bread would soak up some of the acid.

I sat down in the opposite chair from Ms. Mendoza in the living room. As we both gulped our seltzer, I leaned toward her. She slumped in the chair, tired, as if she'd been in the kitchen alongside me, and I smiled. She hiccupped then pointed to the flat screen.

"What's on television, tonight?" she asked.

For the rest of the evening, we watched a cowboy movie featuring one of Argentina's biggest stars, Roberto Escalada. The movie was enjoyable and predictable, but it was nice to have company.

Ms. Mendoza was being more than a neighbor to me, in this moment when I truly needed someone. She was a couple generations apart from mine, but this made her friendship even more important. She was nosy, opinionated, and lived alone, but what more could I ask for? Like fattened heifers, halfway through the movie, on a commercial break, we went back to the kitchen and made ourselves dessert plates. I took some of the coconut cake and a slice of cheesecake. She took a big slice of flan. She reached into my spice rack and took out the cinnamon. That was the ingredient I was conservative in using in the flan. I wasn't sorry she seemed to forget the niceties that new friends usually go through.

I brewed two cups of espresso on the fancy machine Gabriel insisted on purchasing. He could have his stuff back, but he wasn't getting this wonderful contraption. It was too bad he taught me how easy it was to use.

Ms. Mendoza surprised me once again when I walked her home after darkness fell.

"Do you want to come to dinner at my house tomorrow night?" she asked.

"Yes, yes I do," I answered, perhaps a little abruptly but I didn't have any plans for dinner, and I would enjoy the company.

I scrubbed the kitchen with the few ounces of strength I had left. It was harder work than I remembered. When there was nothing left for me to clean, I ran a hot bubble bath and climbed in. I brought with me a novel. I'd never actually read a book in a bathtub before. What kind of life was I living? Bathtub reading was the ultimate relaxing pastime for many film heroines. I couldn't concentrate as well with the bubbles crunching around me and accidentally dipped the pages of the book into the soapy water.

I sat the book on the side of the tub and sucked in a breath. The water engulfed me as I slid my body under the foam. The temperature was just right, and I stayed beneath the water for as long I could hold my breath. When I emerged, my body and thoughts were thoroughly soaked and sleepy. It had been a long day. I slept for thirteen straight hours that night. The longest time I could remember sleeping in a while. Maybe since the first night Gabriel had stayed in my bed.

I woke up around ten a.m. and made myself an espresso. It paired with a decadent and oversized piece of coconut cake, a habit my father indulged in. My parents never held us to proper breakfasts when I was growing up. It didn't hurt as much when my parents came to mind. I was learning to let the memories be.

Chapter Fourteen

A FEW MONTHS AFTER COMING BACK FROM MY LAST KILL WITH Saditha and Gabriel, I checked my messages from Charles and saw a text that read, "Read your email, you know which one."

I logged into my work account and clicked on an email from Charles. It was another photo and a link to a YouTube video from a private account. The photo showed Gianni, Valderron, and Joelle sitting together at my former office, arguing I guessed. It appeared to be taken on a tiny camera in the corner of the room.

Joelle's face was contorted in an ugly expression; she seemed pissed. Great, nothing surprised me at this point. I printed the photograph to examine it again. I clicked on the video and waited for my connection to let me view it in its entirety.

It wasn't a video at all, just audio, and it was labeled with a date. I guessed once I listened to it, some analyst would delete it. It would be nonsense to anyone else who viewed it. I heard the three voices but mostly Gianni. He explained something while shuffling papers. I checked the photos sitting in my printed trail. Joelle had a folder in front of her. This must be what Gianni was shuffling.

"We think Concepcion is alive, Joelle," he said.

Joelle then asked a few obvious questions, but it was good to hear her voice. My battle buddy's voice. Gianni explained the "evidence" he and Valderron had been gathering about my death. The video cut off, no links to other videos. Strange, they always appeared on this site. The cleanup crew didn't do a thorough job with my disappearance. I instantly had the most horrible feeling and whispered, "No, Charles, no."

I dialed Charles in a panic. The lamp in front of me blurred into a rainbow haze. My pulse quickened and I swallowed hard. I took a drink of water from a half-empty bottle. An anxiety attack in the works. I inhaled slowly and breathed out through my nose. I could do this; I could calm myself down. He answered on the third ring.

"You checked your email then," he said, answering with a clipped tone. I shifted my weight on the office chair, bracing myself.

"Yes, of course I did. That's why I'm hyperventilating. Please tell me they are safe, all of them. Alive and well."

"Of course, they are, dear," he said. He didn't elaborate. My suspicions rang true.

"I know they know too much, but they will never find out the truth. I trust your guys did their job well," I said.

"I know they did," he said. "Your friends will not be harmed. Even the agency has its limits."

"Don't give me that shit. You can make one agent disappear," I said. "What about a couple more and another friend who happens to be with them?"

"We don't eliminate just anyone who is doing his job," he said. "They think Aquila did something to you and they can continue thinking that if they choose to do so. It can get no higher up the chain than Aquila, and of course he is aware of your status."

"Oh, make no mistake, Charles, Aquila did many things to me, but I ultimately let everything happen. I let him pull me into this farce about my parents needing me," I said. "What I will not say again is that for no reason whatsoever, including my own personal safety, does anyone in this agency or any other agency ever harm any of them. I will not be a capable agent if my life choices ever affected their lives in a negative way again."

"Okay," he answered.

"Don't make this bitch get ugly," I said.

I said the last sentence not as a threat, because Charles had understood, but as a joke; I wanted to try to lighten up our conversation.

"I'll have to use that line sometime," he said. I could hear the smile in his voice.

"I need to speak with you later about this. While we're on the subject, Aquila might be in your next file. Goodbye."

After we hung up, I lay on the couch and considered my current situation. I'd always wanted a gay buddy to gossip and watch reality shows with, but somehow, I'd resigned myself to the fact that Charles would never be that friend to me. I wondered what Aquila was up to, if he was my next target. He'd lied to me about my parents, no matter what ended up being true.

I wanted to know how Charles came into the agency. I considered what it would be like in ten years if I had a job as a handler. If the money was right, it wouldn't be so difficult. A lot of coordinating back and forth between the headquarters and surveillance teams and people like me, the unmentionables. I would ask about advancement opportunities, but from what I understood, Charles and the others I met were on contract, but we did not have any paperwork on us at the Pentagon. The contracting budget made up a small portion of the CIA budget, but it was a necessary element to maintain a peaceful and carefree existence for the majority of our population.

Charles gave me a few bits of information he'd picked up about the relationship between Joelle and Gianni. My friends broke up. It had only just begun, but what else was new? I had no better luck than her in finding a stable relationship.

Ms. Mendoza had been alone her entire life, and she seemed to have had her version of happiness. She woke up and decided what she wanted to do for the day. Her life was not dictated by her family or any man or woman. A free bird.

The last time he tried to contact me, Gabriel was still trying to cover his tracks.

"I don't think I should apologize for something that wasn't my fault," he had said. "Your jealousy is the problem. I've never been with a passionate woman like you, Sofia. I'm sorry but I was just doing my job."

"I enjoyed you, Gabriel, but I think it was unprofessional what was going on. I can't work that way anymore."

My words did not match my heart, but they rarely did in a life where lying was breathing.

What I saw was too much to pretend that it wouldn't happen again. This was a job that meant by any means necessary. Apparently, he'd poisoned her with seafood and was in the process of taking away her oxygen when I came up and shot her. His perfect plan was spoiled, and his career was at risk because of the number of people that had seen the two together.

He could have claimed anaphylactic shock and, if caught, convinced the police he had just met the woman, and he would have been home free. After everything, though, he still wanted to be with me. I didn't want to mix business with pleasure. It brought out the crazy in me.

"One more thing, Sofia. And I'm not sure what this means, but a guy approached me at our Washington office. He gave me a message in person: 'Tell your girlfriend that her parents are going to die, no matter what she does.' I thought your parents were dead, and I'm not sure you ever agreed to be my girlfriend."

I feigned ignorance because what could I do. I didn't tell Charles what Gabriel said about my parents. They were an enigma to me, with a racing clock on a timeline I was not a part of. Saving them would mean what to me at this point, if they were even alive? A normal life? What did that look like? Life was this until I met the service end of a weapon.

Charles sent Gabriel back to Southeast Asia for a post in Thailand. I was sure he'd be really busy there. He could enjoy as many women as he could pay. Without him in front of me, it was easier to make him a distant memory. It was a big wide world out there, and there would be someone else to warm my bed. I was not cold-hearted. I told Charles not to hurt him intentionally. He agreed.

I spent the day dancing the tango with Ms. Mendoza and her slew of seasoned white-haired dancers. She looked twenty years younger in her dancing costumes. She moved gracefully across the polished wooden floor where we spent afternoons. I learned all the ballroom steps; Ms. Mendoza surprisingly had the stamina to teach me.

At the studio, she had a poster-sized framed photograph of a striking young man. It was recent and stood out from the other minimalist decorations on the light blue walls.

"Who's that dancer on the poster? He looks like he melted a few hearts," I said. He was a similar stature as my neighbor.

"Are you sure you're Argentinian, girl?" she said. I shrugged my shoulders. "That's Herman Cornejo. One of the top ballerinos in the history of the world. He's in New York now but he is from Buenos Aires. Herman is a national treasure, a symbol for us that we can compete with the world in dance, specifically ballet."

I stared at the poster and considered my lack of knowledge about basic things in my new culture. I was going to look him up and try to understand the million ways Ms. Mendoza could uncover my secret. The experience I'd gained as an American, a soldier, didn't help me here. It was a liability.

During my hours in the studio, I perfected my cumbia style and taught a few high school girls who tagged along with their grandmothers. I was most comfortable with the kind of dance they could go into a club and show off to their friends. Ms. Mendoza didn't approve of my own lessons, mostly because she was supposed to be the head instructor of all amateurs. I didn't want her title. I just liked to dance.

I got up off the sofa and went back to the computer to try and replay the video link. "This video has been removed by the user," appeared on the screen where the video once was. I was a little disappointed. I wanted to hear the conversation again to see if I could pick up any clues; mostly I wanted to hear three of my former friends talk about me.

It reminded me of how much Concepcion was loved. I wasn't her anymore. I was Sofia. I had changed in the past year and some months. My life didn't feel like such a rat race. In addition to no sex recently, I hadn't received any contracts from Charles. Maybe it was intentional, and my handler wanted to keep me out of the game for a while, and I couldn't complain.

This job took an extreme amount of precision and control. I was still in my head so much. I couldn't become more of a risk.

I went back to the photograph. It seemed like Valderron and Gianni had ganged up on Joelle with that file. I didn't know what could possibly be inside, but Joelle wasn't visibly shocked. Maybe Joelle had considered the idea all along. She did have a way with these kinds of things. She couldn't take anything at face value. It must have been the same self-preservation instincts that kept her clear of many messes in Iraq, or even when we came back home.

The update wasn't a good one. I enjoyed the idea of Joelle and Gianni being a couple, but somehow, they had managed to screw it up.

I needed to get out of my house and do something productive. I called Ms. Mendoza and asked what her plans were for the day.

"I will be home working in the garden, but you are welcome to come over and weed if you want," she said, and I pictured her sitting by the old phone in the kitchen.

"Definitely, I'll be over," I said. It wasn't anything I hadn't done before. I threw on a pair of knee length yoga pants so the creepy crawlers couldn't crawl up my pants and grabbed a pair of work gloves from underneath the sink.

I walked the few paces over to her yard and found Ms. Mendoza sitting in the dirt on her hands and knees. She wore a pair of thick knee pads designed for rollerblading because of her bursitis on the caps of her knees. I didn't want to think about getting any older than I was, but Ms. Mendoza made it less scary. She put one foot in front of the other and kept on living. I had a sense that she had more tragedy in her life than she ever let on. I was curious but decided to let her be. I didn't need any reminders of the horrible things mankind was capable of doing.

The dirtier and sweatier I became, the better I felt. I weeded her flower garden and the areas lining the house for close to two hours.

"You better take a break, senora," I said. "It's hot as Hades out here."

"This is what keeps me young, you know," she said. "I have to stay busy, or I might die just like these roses."

She pointed to a bush that wasn't getting enough sunshine and looked a bit droopy, more than the rest.

"I'll only take a break if you'll stay for dinner. I'm fixing something extra special. We do need something sweet for dessert," she said, in our familiar way. We often assumed the other one was coming for dinner.

I appreciated when she gave me some way to contribute to the meal. I was getting used to having her as a steady companion.

She didn't feel the need to spy on me anymore.

"I'll go to the bakery," I said, standing up and stretching my limbs.

"Go to the new one near the shopping center. It's got the best tortas," she called after me before she went inside, carrying all her tools with her, setting a trowel and watering can on her back steps.

She didn't have a garden shed like I did. I wondered if for her birthday next month, she would let me have one built for her. I threw my gloves on the kitchen counter and grabbed my purse. I could shower later. I didn't want to get back too late if she was fixing dinner. She became grouchy if she didn't eat on her schedule. She preferred to eat hours before I ever got hungry, but all the gardening made me able to eat early.

I pulled onto my street and gunned the engine towards Ms. Mendoza's burning three-story villa. Flames engulfed the first floor and I cried out, "No!" I grabbed my phone and dialed to get help on the way, try to do something.

"Hello, what is your emergency?" the operator said, in a bored tone.

"Fire!" I screamed into the phone, and then choked on my words. "Fire." I couldn't think past that.

"There is a fire? Where, ma'am?"

I quickly processed the situation and rattled off the address. Her question brought me briefly out of my panicked state.

"There is an elderly woman possibly inside," I said, as I scanned the scene for any sign of her. "Please hurry."

The fire was engulfing the second floor. I got out of my car and screamed at the orange and red fireball.

"Help! Ms. Mendoza!" I said, to no one in particular. "Where are you? Are you outside?"

Did she get out in time? I couldn't see anyone. It was only six in the evening. Why was the street so empty? I thought back to the traffic jams in the city. There was a huge Argentinian football star from the World Champion Italian National Team, Mauro Camoranesi, signing autographs at the shopping center, which might have caused delays. Standing on the street, I looked behind me and saw an older lady on her porch. She was a friend of Ms. Mendoza's. I called out to her, but she couldn't hear me with the crackling and popping noise of the flaming house. The fire was spreading while I cried out to my friend. If she wasn't dead by now, she would be soon. I pushed away the gravity of what her death would mean.

"No, don't leave me, don't leave me," I mumbled to myself.

I was useless. It was out of my hands. The house was kindling now.

The fire raged in full force, and by the time the fire trucks arrived, twelve minutes later, it had spread to the Paltrini villa. The heat of the flames warmed my face, but I couldn't run away. I sobbed in the street while the captain of the team dispersed the men. Someone came over to me and pulled me back from the scene. I didn't resist but I was numb.

Everything I had built for myself, carved out of nothing, was burning up in front of me. I cared nothing for the houses; I only cared about my friend. She was making our dinner not even an hour before. I cried and cried, while the men worked on stopping the fire. There was nothing to be done. It eventually engulfed the side of my home before the crew was able to put it out. It was useless now. I couldn't imagine a worse way to go. My only hope was that she died from smoke inhalation and was gone before the flames took her. That was my prayer. That was what I asked God to reassure me happened. I had to get out of the street, but I could not think of where to go. I sobbed like I had never sobbed before. I couldn't remember crying for anyone else besides my own parents.

There was so much I still wanted to know about her life, so much she could teach me about living. I had led a vain, selfish, damaged existence, and the past months with her, I thought I saw something good inside myself again. I wanted to be a productive person and become something more substantive than a killer. I had discovered many other ways to fill my day than planning and executing another person's death. I got back a little of the girl who had such a bright future before her parents died. I could leave the agency someday and carve out a life in the real world. It was possible.

Ms. Mendoza never understood what I was, and she would never know the truth about me. I leaned against the iron fence of one of the homes on our street, holding onto something solid while my world crumbled around me. More death. Always more death. Especially now.

A police officer came over to me and escorted me to his car. He was a large, balding man, fat really, but he looked strong and fatherly as he took in my appearance with his soft brown eyes. He seemed to understand the gravity before he asked me a question. I began instead. I wanted to get it over with.

"To me, her name is Ms. Elma Mendoza. We were together working in the garden all afternoon and we planned on having dinner tonight together," I stopped and tried to continue speaking. It was too much.

"When did the fire start?"

"I don't know. I went to the confiterías, and she went inside to finish cooking. When I got here the first floor was burning and I was the only one here."

"How long did you know the victim?" he asked. "A good friend to you?"

I physically could not answer the man, only let the tears flow. I flashed to the silence of the street as my friend and her home were destroyed in front of me.

There was no sense to any of it. No sense at all. I cried for

Ms. Mendoza, and I didn't stop for the sake of the police who still talked amongst themselves about what to do with me. For a moment, maybe longer, I wasn't certain of anything.

I saw the bodies of women and children covered in shrapnel, the grotesque positions of their limbs and body parts. The soldiers' grim faces and the emptiness in their eyes. I closed my eyes and stayed in the hell I had lived through. It gave me pleasure to relive the horrors of my life, only because I was so sad, and I wanted to be dead with all the rest. I let my anxiety and my panic take hold, and I yelled out to the police in my native language. I saw my hand take the Gerber knife and continuously stab the senator's son in the sand. I shook my smallish hands that killed so many after him. Planned and in cold blood. I was a monster. My grip on the edges of sanity loosened, and I let myself go. I relaxed my shoulders and dropped my head, staring at the pavement.

"Kill me please. Help me please, help me. I want to die," I said in English. I had sealed my fate.

"I am Concepcion Chapa, an American agent under cover as one of your own citizens," I said. "Call Joelle McCoy, she will tell you who I am. Call my parents and tell them I am dead."

They had to take charge of me now. I pleaded with them to kill me because I was tired of living in any existence. I couldn't live a lie anymore.

"I have been a bad, bad person," I said. "I killed too many people to live."

Chapter Fifteen

I WOKE UP IN A HOSPITAL BED, DRUGGED. IT WAS NIGHT AND IT looked like I was still in Buenos Aires, the skyline of the city all lit up through my window.

It was a private room. That meant Charles had something to do with me being here. Otherwise I would be in less accommodating quarters. I debated pushing the red button just inches from my hand. They wanted me to push it. I had an infusion tube, an IV, sticking out of my right arm.

I decided to call the nurse. If I was supposed to be dead, Charles would have done it by now. I had gone rogue and lived, at least for now, to tell about it. Under what circumstances could I possibly have been brought here instead of a jail cell? With all my ranting and raving, it could have been presumed that I had started the fire. There were no other witnesses, and I must have appeared certifiably insane.

I pushed the call button. The nurse came in, and I decided to play along. I noticed she brought something resembling a meal with her.

I asked why I was there and what was wrong with me.

She hesitated and, instead of answering me, she spooned soup into my mouth. It tasted salty and vaguely resembled beef broth. I ate what she served me. No use in making it worse for myself by giving the nurse problems.

Before she left, she turned, smiled, and said, "You have a visitor who has been here since last night when you came in."

It was Charles. He came in looking like a dissolved version of his usually neat self. He hadn't shaved and would have looked more handsome with the beard if his eyes weren't so harried.

"You came," I managed to say. For now, it was enough. He feigned a smile.

"Of course, I came. I brought you here for treatment of your condition," he said.

"And what condition is that?" I said, returning to my usual sarcastic wit. "I had better memorize the symptoms before the doctor comes in."

"Oh, you didn't know. I am your doctor, your psychiatrist to be more precise. You had a traumatic episode and needed medical attention," he said. I played along.

"You didn't answer my first question, what is my condition?"

"Oh, that's easy, post-traumatic stress disorder. I always thought a lie sounded more believable when it had a bit of truth in it," he said.

"The real question, Charles," I said, as I took his hand and made direct eye contact while he stood over my bed.

Did he understand what I was about to ask him? "Will I live?"

"Yes, you will," he said, holding my gaze.

"Are you sure? But, what I did? What I said?"

"What did you say? Because no one understood your gibberish over the fire trucks and police sirens wailing, but as far as what you yourself remember saying? I am your only judge and jury, and I tell you, Miss Paltrini, that you will live."

"I am a liability... I honestly couldn't control myself," I whispered. I couldn't believe I was making a case for my own elimination, but I was. It was too much of a burden to bear, and I had nothing else to lose.

"Actually, what happened was a completely normal response. It is only a matter of time for the sort of people who do your job. You don't think your incident was the first or last for this agency, do you?"

I adjusted myself in the bed. I had been bathed. My skin was itchy like sunburn, but I didn't have any external injuries, as far as I could tell. Charles sat in a chair at the foot of the bed. He looked exhausted.

"I had the worst dream, Charles," I murmured. I had to release this energy. "She...came to me. And then I saw my parents, but they weren't like her. She told me to run and..."

Charles cut me off with a wave of his hand. "Not now, darling, but I promise I will hear all about it."

I thought of the flames covering Ms. Mendoza, and then how I felt after I was told my parents died. My friend had come to me in a dream, and something deep inside me understood she had died the most terrible death. But I couldn't sense my parents. She was so near to me, but not them. She was warm and they were cold. What could it mean? I was confused and raw from the experience.

"What's next for us, Charles?" I said, "My home is half-gone and I don't think I can go back there...after everything that has happened."

"Right now, you will stay here for the night, before we decide what you want to do next."

"Thank you, Charles," I practically shouted to him. I wasn't hurt, just tired.

"Don't thank me yet, Miss Paltrini," he said. "We still have many details to go over."

I waved to him as he left. The idea of a new assignment, a

new location, took the place of yesterday's hellish nightmare. It made me happy to consider another new beginning. I hoped I got to stay Miss Paltrini because I couldn't learn another language, or another accent, for that matter. Would I still be an assassin? Would I completely change my position?

Both ideas worried me. I had to get control over my anxiety. I hoped whatever was in the IV gave me back my bearings. If Charles had told someone above his pay grade that one of his agents had PTSD resulting from a friend's death, they would probably be confused, but would maybe grant me a change of assignment. Or maybe it was our little secret.

I could never tell with Charles. In my heart, I was grateful to him. Only in my darkest hour did I realize how understanding and kind he was to me. I was sure that the stunt I pulled would be a bullet to the back of my head, but he took care of me instead. I cried for Ms. Mendoza because Charles had said that was a normal response to a traumatic event. I'd killed many people in my life with a coldness surrounding my heart, but I wasn't all stone. I grieved for my friend. She would be missed. I was tired of losing the ones I loved.

The following morning, I walked out of the hospital with Charles. He brought me clean, new clothes; there was no sign of the ones I had worn in the garden just days before. On the outside, I looked good as new, but we both knew that I was anything but healed.

Charles drove us away in the silver Acura sedan. I didn't ask where we were going. I was just along for the ride. He drove in silence, and, after we left the highly trafficked area of down-town, Charles put the radio on. It was a reggae station. He didn't seem like the Don Omar type, but he left the dial alone, so I sang along.

I'd listened to the Puerto Rican rapper since I was a teenager. His lyrics were harsh and represented a world I was grateful to be away from, far from the suburbs of Miami where Chantrea and Jimm lived. The song reminded me of being young, when there were only question marks in my future.

As we drove into the countryside of Argentina, I thought about how the only thing that had really stayed the same in my life was enjoying this song. I was still a young woman, but I had done very mature, criminal things. I would never be free of all my burdens, no matter how much I lied to the world.

I didn't sing loudly until the chorus. It was a simple repeat-ing phrase, and Charles repeated it with me with his horrible Spanish pronunciation. He was supposed to sound British, and he did. I could be going anywhere, and Charles could kill me, but I had been reminded that I wanted to live. My past wasn't all death and destruction. There were some good parts too. As if he was reading my mind, Charles interrupted the thumping music.

"Joelle is doing well. She doesn't send her regards or anything, but she is doing well."

"Is she back with Gianni or what?" I asked, curious about her love life.

"Not sure but she did change the cell phone number we were tracking her on. We don't have cause to find out her new one. She is still in Missouri, and he is still based out of Miami."

"You don't need to find out anymore," I said. "I think she will be alright no matter what craziness I brought her into."

"Okay, then no more surveillance," he said. "I am sure the crews will have plenty of other cases to attend to."

"Did they keep searching for me?" I asked. I figured I might as well find out while Charles was being candid.

"Gianni and your ex-boyfriend still seem to be collecting bits and pieces, but Aquila assured us they haven't brought up anything to anyone besides Joelle."

"One more question, and I understand if you can't answer it. Does Aquila still work for us?"

He worked closely with the Department of Homeland Security on many of the cases our team had been assigned to, but I didn't know if he worked directly for the agency.

"I think it's obvious, and I am actually surprised you asked. The answer is no, and the only important business he ever conducted with us was giving us a lead into your willingness to join up. He was close to your parents, and their legacy has cemented his position. He worked with the CIA through the FBI because, abroad, specifically in South America, we have always worked together. He's a bit of a wanker and not the kind to work well with us. Anything high level with the Bureau is routed around, away from Aquila. He is working in some dangerous territory now, but I don't have the details on it. We were given some information that he tried to contact our team in an unauthorized, potentially illegal way. He is a liability, but he did help us find you. I might even get my hands dirty with that job. He fucked you over."

"Because he lied to me about my parents."

"No, I don't think so."

"Don't do this to me again," I brushed a few stray strands of hair out of my face. "I'm clinging to my last little bit of sanity."

"I'm honestly telling you now that I have met two people that are supposedly your parents," he glanced over at me. "It was five or six years ago in Azerbaijan, and we had a joint mission. I stayed back as an intelligence officer while they were in the field. We called them 'the Argentines' as a code name. Your alleged mother was very unassuming, pretty but not beautiful. She spoke quietly to her partner, your father, who called or wrote the reports. I remember that they spoke Farsi to one another, and that detail was odd. They were very private, not showy, and left with a small group of five other team members."

"Why haven't you told me any of this? I've been driving myself crazy trying to understand why I am here."

"My orders changed. Originally, after training, you were supposed to join the group of five to help them locate your parents. But then..." He hesitated and his body froze up. I nodded for him to continue.

"But then they came back. Just walked into our Singapore office and got back to work like nothing happened. During the debrief, the team gave them an update on your activation status. They declined to have you on the team. It wasn't what they wanted for you."

As he drove, I looked out the window and fidgeted with my purse handle. I closed my eyes to try and understand exactly how all of this had played out.

"And so...what was the order then? After your lot royally fucked up my life using my parents as bait."

"Well, that's the part I'm not proud of. The Gabriel thing was supposed to help you. Your parents don't know we kept you on as a CIA officer. We couldn't undo what we already did. In this line of work, it's hard to go back. You were really good. You were the prodigy child of these two all-stars in the intelligence community. We wanted you. *I* wanted you on my team. I made the case to keep you on. We couldn't just up-end your life and say never mind."

"Do you really think they are my parents?" I asked, the knowledge of my situation sinking in.

"Yes, I do."

"How can you be so sure?"

"Because they didn't want you in this life. That's the most parental choice I have witnessed."

"What if they are imposters?"

"That's not a possibility. They built that team and asked the same aging senators for fifty years for funding. There is something like a yearbook that the CIA kept on the team, without their knowledge of course. I saw it a few times, and the one thing I took away from their photos was a certain sadness, an emptiness. But they had each other. That must be enough."

"Enough," I whispered. "Good for them."

I thought about the choices my parents had and all the choices I didn't get to make for myself. I stared in my lap at hands, some of the last parts of me unchanged by surgery.

The blood on my hands was my own. I had to bear what I became. No more of them, no more excuses, no more victim. I came back to myself. I turned into a victim when I remembered losing my mother and my father. I lost a reflection of both the feminine and the masculine versions of myself as we aged. I couldn't understand parents that would leave a child permanently. I witnessed mothers on deployment who had no choice. They cried for hours, cashing out thousands of dollars in phone cards just to hear their kid's voice.

The love of a mother was supposed to be the purest of all types of love. When my parents disappeared out of my life, by choice or not, I had all the parenting I was going to get. Withdrawn, I protected the best parts of me, the seeker, the dreamer, the creator. The vulnerable kid who remained wrapped up in their memories was emerging, free of my cocoon to face the facts. I wasn't enough.

Charles touched my hand.

"I'm not going to leave you ignorant on this. I received permission to show you their own cases from old files. I'm leaving it with you once we get settled. I think it can give you some context about who they are. I'm doing this because I want you to get through this. You're too good. But it's up to you if you actually read it."

"Yeah, I will. It's all I have left really."

The details finally rang true. My skin tingled and burned from the new information. My thoughts cascaded like a waterfall of loss. I missed my friend. I missed my life.

We drove away for about nine hours until we hit a checkpoint for Chile. We both showed our IDs, an Argentinian and a British passport. Just a couple of lovebirds going on a mini vacation. "What is your business in Chile?" the man asked.

"Pleasure, just seeing the Incan ruins," I answered, leaning over Charles's lap.

We had discussed what to say but I hesitated slightly. Charles nodded right alongside me like what I had said was the gospel truth. Once we passed through the checkpoint, we stopped to get gas and take a break. I wasn't sure when we would eat. I bought a protein shake and an apple.

I needed to keep my energy up, and I had put on a little

weight in the past few months. My body was damaged from the chaos and the frenetic pace. I was determined to build a wall around the damage and come out someone different. A new beginning, over and over again. With a clean slate, I wanted to be in fighting shape. It was something that Charles wanted even when my own parents did not. It made me proud to be in the CIA. My thoughts were shifting, and I needed to take my next assignment with the same vigor I'd started with. The weight had come on little by little, meal by meal with my friendly neighbor.

I still went to the gym regularly but based on experience, I understood my diet was the most important factor in maintaining my shapely, tightly muscled figure. We rode along with the radio tuned to a different station playing the same style of music.

The landscape of the mountainous Chile flew by as Charles steered the vehicle round and around, climbing higher and higher. The road itself was thin by any stretch of the imagination. I rolled down the windows to let in the fresh air. As we got closer and closer to the top of the ridge, the homes became much more elaborate. We finally came to a house built high into the bluff, a dangerous drop but expansive majestic views for anyone brave enough to go to the edge. Charles cut the engine near the entrance to the home and pulled the emergency break into position.

"Where are we, my kind sir?" I asked.

"Just a little place I like to call my home away from home."

Besides the view, the mountainside served as a natural foundation for the three-story brownstone structure. It stood out from the other grand houses we had seen on the drive up because the deep rich color contrasted with its green surroundings.

It was not discreet. It made a statement in a country I knew so little about. It had been a long road trip when I hadn't expected to drive so far, but now that we were here, I stretched my arms overhead and leaned forward in the direction of the evening sun.

Charles unloaded a small suitcase, which seemed funny as he wheeled it up the pebble-stone pathway. I could see myself living in the solitude of these mountains, except that I hated the cold. I doubted Charles stayed here often because it was so remote. He had to be close to all the action for his job. This would be a nice escape for the few weeks we each took as some sort of break.

I followed him to the entrance. He held the door open for me. The inside of the first level was merely a marble staircase leading up to three separate levels. I hadn't guessed from the outside, but three different people could potentially live on the premises.

We went into the first wooden door with a heavy wood frame. Large, open glass windows let light into the marble hallway. The house had the same pink, black, and grey color as the entrance, and marble floors throughout. It was carefully designed with a minimalist eye. A man's house, with a masculine feel to it.

I followed the staircase to Charles's bedroom. I didn't step inside, but I looked at him for some direction.

He caught my stare. Charles was impossibly handsome, and when he looked into my eyes, I held my breath. If only he wasn't gay. Sometimes I caught him looking a little longer than necessary, but nothing happened. Pull it together, girl.

"Your room is around the corner, near the kitchen. It has its own bathroom joined to it opposite the closet. I left a few necessary items you'll need for your stay."

"Thank you, Charles," I said. "It's lovely."

"Only the best for you," he replied.

I walked into the guest bedroom. A large replica of a Frida Kahlo painting hung above the bed. It seemed like the most fun color palate, different from the rest of the house. The glass door led out to a terrace facing the sunset. The first level was not flush with the ground, but it wouldn't be a far fall.

I opened the door to let in the fresh air. Air conditioning the huge house would take a lot of energy. It was conveniently a comfortable seventy degrees outside. The bed was covered with a pretty burgundy quilt, the rest of the bed made up. The dresser included a large mirror, and I dared to look at myself. My browned skin, shiny from the car ride, and my forehead slightly wrinkled, but otherwise my ordeal from two days before was not evident in my appearance.

I looked at my eyes because that was where all my secrets would hide from the rest of the world. They knew all about me.

I blinked several times at my reflection; I would have to do a better job hiding my damaging past. I was good at starting over, or decent at lying to myself about it. I opened the dresser drawers and found sized underwear in my size, a modest biki-ni-cut, covering more than my typical thong panties, but maybe Charles wanted to start me out more fully clothed. It could get chilly here up in the mountains. The rest of the drawer came fully stocked with pajamas, jeans, and workout pants.

A "Santiago te ama" T-shirt was in the drawer as well. At least he had a sense of humor. I closed the dresser drawers and went to see the rest of his home.

He was in the kitchen, opening and closing doors to the pantry and surveying their contents. Maybe he had someone else do the shopping. He turned to me when I stepped inside the kitchen. It was tiny in comparison to the rest of the house. Its builder must not have considered the home's most important feature.

"How did you find your room?" he asked.

"I found it well, thank you."

As if in reaction to his accent, my own vocabulary always improved the more I hung around my boss.

"I would have liked a few different clothing choices, but beggars can't be choosers." I smiled as I said it. I was being a smart ass. That was a good sign. Inside of myself, I was very grateful that I wasn't in charge anymore. For the past six months, I had been laying low and became complacent with my life in Buenos Aires.

The fire reminded me how fast anyone's life could change, and I should have prepared for any disaster. It shook me to the core. I needed to build myself back up to where I could be of some use to my employer.

"What would you like for dinner tonight?" he asked after he selected several options from the fully-stocked pantry.

"Got anything not so full of carbohydrates and sodium?" I asked. "Instead of dried pasta and white rice? I followed a Mediterranean diet before I gorged myself with Mendoza at all hours of the night. I miss her."

"Sure, we can select some frozen seafood I have in the freezer," he said.

Dinner was a grilled fish and mix of colored veggies. It hit the spot, and I felt more comfortable with our diet choices. If I stayed here for any length of time, I needed to go shopping. Charles prepared a plate of pasta with olive oil and garlic for himself. The scent filled the whole house but with all the doors opened to the outside, I hoped the smell of dinner wouldn't linger.

We had a bottle of Prosecco with the meal. Charles always had a wealth of rich liquors and wine.

"How long will I be staying here?" I asked, after I had eaten just enough to settle my stomach.

"It's up to you, love," he said.

Twirling the remaining dry wine in his glass, he was memorizing and quick to answer. I had never seen this man so relaxed. This was his home. I liked this answer.

"Where else would I go?" I asked. "Any career plans for me?"

"I thought I told you earlier," he said, as he sipped his wine. "I will provide you with a list of possibilities and you can decide, with my approval of course."

"Okay, well, can you at least tell me where we are in this country?" I asked. "Then maybe I can decide where I want to go next. Maybe I can stay here with you forever."

Standing up, Charles started to collect the empty dishes. His silence after my last comment made me nervous.

"It *is* beautiful, isn't it," Charles said as he loaded the dishwasher with our dinner plates. "We are in the central part of Chile, near the harbor city of Valparaiso. It's the city that you see from the right side of my house."

I'd guessed that after our trip from Buenos Aires, we would head to another metropolitan area, and I was partially right. I knew Valparaiso was one of the country's major cities outside of the capital, Santiago.

The population out here wasn't as congested as in Buenos Aires or Santiago, and maybe that was why Charles picked this location. Every new city took time to adjust to, and I was still dealing with my own demons. I would explore the city, but I doubted the agency needed a huge presence here.

Chile was a stable country considering the rest of the continent. Though the size of the Argentinian population made it a considerably better choice to house agents like me.

I walked the rest of the first floor with Charles as he showed me where I could watch TV or check my email.

"*Mi casa es su casa*," he said, as he motioned for me to take in his stellar taste in art, which lined the walls. I wasn't buying that he picked it out.

"Are you the only one who lives here?"

"Yes, and no," he said, answering me like he had been expecting the question. "The third floor is a state-of-the-art home gym, and it is considerably smaller than the first floor.

"The second floor..." he hesitated but continued. "The second floor is my partner's area, but he is in The Netherlands at the moment on business."

"*Partner* as in the business, or personal sense?"

"Personal, and we live virtually separate lives because of our work. He knows you will be staying with me and apologized he wouldn't get to meet you to show you around his city," he said.

Charles seemed more open than I had ever seen him after his car ride confession, though that was mainly work. I wondered what triggered his sudden openness.

I had always been honest with Charles, but I didn't have much of a choice, what with my personal life affecting the agency. He had to know what his assigned agents were up to because that was his job.

"So, your partner is from the area?" I asked. I wanted to keep the focus on this mystery man if he would allow. I needed a distraction; otherwise, I might remember why I was here.

"Yes, he grew up in Valparaiso and is usually here more than me, but he is attending an art auction. He is a buyer for an art house in Santiago and another one from the local area. Depending on how long you stay, you may get to meet him."

"I would like that, Charles," I said. Though he was a stuffy Brit, I went up and wrapped my arms around his trim waist. He towered over me, but he politely hugged back.

"Thank you, for everything, boss."

Back in my room, he dropped a stack of folders labeled *classified* on my nightstand.

"As you wish," he said. "It's a lot but it's the truth."

I stared back, wide-eyed and perplexed. The CIA telling me the truth?

"Got it. I'll read it someday but not right now."

I slept through the night thanks to the sedative Charles gave me, grateful for a temporary reprieve and some much-needed REM.

Chapter Sixteen

DURING MY FIRST FEW DAYS IN VALPARAISO, I DID WHAT ANY tourist would do. I rode the ascensores, the cable cars, all over the hilly city. Charles had his own activities planned. I guessed it had something to do with Sergio, his partner. That was why he dropped me off at an art dealer's shop in Vina del Mar. I didn't have any problem finding my way to the small, well stocked clothing stores. In each place I bought clothing, I never decided on a style of dress until I saw what all the other women my age considered the latest fashion.

Valparaiso seemed to have its own personal style, like every city I visited. It was well-known for its art scene, and most buildings were brightly colored and resembled a version of the famous Cinque Terre in Italy. The difference in this city was all the graffiti, illegal or approved. The streets dazzling as an open-air museum, called Museo a Cielo Abierto, and I stopped to observe several doors in the Atahualpa lane, each one styled by a different artist. Eventually, I found a Sandra Alvarez store and decided the mannequins in the window best represented what the women around me were wearing. I bought a few bags worth.

The clothes made me feel a bit younger, and I couldn't recall seeing a black colored item in the whole store. I noticed everyone was wearing boots—leather, calf-length boots that usually matched the skirts and dresses, almost like a cowgirl style. Instead of my usual arm full of stiletto shoes boxes, I bought three different kinds of boots, all designer brands from Italy. Who was I kidding? I also bought a couple of stilettos.

New shoes, new me. I called Charles from a little café that catered to the starving artist types. A chalk board sign out front read "don't trust your tour guide."

"Great advice!" I said, as I walked through the open door.

I wanted to kick back on the sofa at my temporary home, Charles's place and take a much-needed nap, but he still had business.

"Why don't you take the cable car two streets over to Calle Vittro and see if you can get in to see Paco for a salon appointment?" he asked.

I followed Charles's suggestion to the letter and walked to the shop, which was on a side street. Another sign next to it made me smile, this one was painted on the side of the building. "We are not hippies, we are happies." It was all about the kitsch here.

I easily spotted Paco, the only man in a shop full of women in various states of transformation.

"I want a change," I said, as I sat in his chair. "You pick the cut and color."

The first thing I noticed about Paco was that he was prettier than me.

"I always do," he said, as he looked back at me and winked.

I relaxed in the chair and read *Hola*, a gossip magazine with the trashiest of headlines. Many Latino celebrities came from South America and I enjoyed reading the extended cover of their affairs, sex scandals, and baby bump photos.

When my color was almost done, Paco kneaded my shoulders. I appreciated his nimble fingers loosening up my muscles.

Carrying all my new purchases could be considered weightlifting so I mentally crossed off an evening workout from my plans.

"Ay, Paco," I said, practically purring with delight. "You must get all the boys with those fingers."

"You got it all wrong, Miss Argentina," he said plainly. "I don't give the boys massages," he said. "They take care of me. I am the one who stands all day making everyone look glamorous."

I liked his attitude. I had the feeling we would be great friends if I decided to hang around in the city. I had to find out more about this guy and how Charles maintained a long-distance relationship with Sergio. I was curious if Paco would have the scoop on Charles.

Besides the fact that Paco was a local hairstylist and Charles was a British CIA man, they were opposites in another way. Paco was flamboyantly gay and Charles on most days could be straight. I thought about his partner, Sergio. Did Sergio know who Charles worked for?

I had not dated a civilian since I entered the military. I always picked the guys who could understand what I meant when I said I had a hell of a day. There were no off switches or punch cards when it came to the military lifestyle, the FBI, and, naturally, the CIA.

Sometimes I envied the lifestyles of people who could leave their work at the office; mine followed me around everywhere. I *was* my job. Could I do any other? Could I be happy doing anything different? I'd lived through three career changes, each more dangerous than the last. I'd found the ultimate high-risk, high paying, thrilling career, but when would I say enough is enough? What had this career cost me and for what gain? When would money not matter? This couldn't be about my country anymore. The one I couldn't return to unless I had a permission slip from the agency.

While Paco rinsed my color and snipped away at my freshly washed hair, I watched the strands fall at a frenetic pace. He was giving me a much shorter look than I was used to seeing on myself. I reminded myself it was just hair. It was the only dead thing that kept growing in my life.

I could always order more fake hair from Brazil. The guy who sold me the last package would probably wonder what I did with it all.

I could write, "Please send me the same colors I ordered last time, it caught on fire and now I am bald."

Paco spun me around to face the mirror. I looked very different. Chic to death, but not me. I had bangs, cut perfectly straight just above my eyes and the color—a warm chocolate brown, with honey-kissed highlights framing my layered chin-length cut.

The new haircut made me an *Hola! Glamour* girl. My dark eyebrows were now the same chocolate brown as my hair. I looked like a woman with a fresh start. Paco stood behind me. He didn't ask what I thought, he told me instead.

"You love it, I know," he said, his eyes transfixed on his work. "Miss Argentina takes out her ponytail and now joins the rest of the young sexy women of this country."

My brown eyes popped with my new color and my skin appeared darker, healthier.

I paid Paco handsomely and had him point me in the direction of the closest bookstore. It was within walking distance but going up the hills was easier said than done. The altitude changed from one hill to the next and I was sweating within a few minutes.

My head felt lighter after everything Paco cut off. I had a similar haircut right before Joelle and I deployed together. Strange to think I wouldn't be hearing about her life anymore; even as a third party it was grounding to see how she was doing. I doubted she would spend all the money I gave her foolishly, but I didn't need to keep tabs on her anymore. She had her life and I had mine.

About three hills from the salon, I found the little shop on a corner near a large ice cream shop. If I wasn't watching my weight, I would have gone there first. I'd left all my shopping bags at the salon with Paco so I wouldn't have to haul them around with me.

When I placed them in his care, Paco gave me a slight smile. If he had any drag tendencies, he might try to squish his feet into my boots, or, even more hilarious, my stilettos.

I was concerned for no more than a moment. Walking into the bookstore, my nose was flooded with the scent of new books. The outside of the city did not smell the greatest, but the bookstore, with air conditioning and coffee brewing for the owner, made me breathe a lot easier. I was sweating my ass literally off up a hill.

I found the Coelho book easily. My other copy of *Eleven Minutes* was left in the wreckage of my villa. I couldn't let myself think about Ms. Mendoza.

Out of habit, I spun an antique globe lining one of the shelves. It spun slowly at the light touch of my fingertips. I could go anywhere at this point. If I wanted to get out of the agency, I could flee this life completely and start again. But I wasn't strong enough or crazy enough to venture out on my own without the approval of my government. I still felt beholden to the notion that going AWOL, or "Absent Without Leave," was one of the things forbidden by the ten commandants, and probably the only such edict I followed.

Thou shalt not kill had its own place, with my many caveats and addendums added to it. In my case, though shalt not kill unless I was paid to do it by my government.

Joelle wouldn't sanction my way of life even if her Army background gave her the experience to surrender to something greater than herself. But this was beyond service, beyond sacrifice. She had been right to get out. The matters of right and wrong were not black and white. She wouldn't survive the guilt of killing other human beings continuously and firing at will. Killing on command was a mindset for many soldiers, good and bad ones alike.

I stopped the spinning globe and my fingers touched somewhere in the Indian Ocean. I wouldn't go anywhere near there. That was certain heartbreak for me. I brought my purchase up to the counter where an older, bald man with round, wire-rimmed glasses was watching my approach. He was reading a newspaper. I wondered if he could tell I wasn't from the area. It was my second attempt at reading the book. The fire would have given me a good excuse not to continue, but what else was I doing in Chile? I couldn't gorge myself on local cuisine. I was determined to study and train.

The man scanned the price tag on my book and waited for me to pull out my newly purchased wallet, stuffed full of cash Charles had given me.

"Miss, have you read any other of Coelho's works?" he asked.

"Yes, I just started reading his books. I enjoyed *The Alchemist* and one other," I said.

"Oh, but you need to read *The Pilgrimage* before this one, and *Brida* as well," he said. He came around from his side of the counter and motioned for me to follow his lead.

I followed him back to the shelf where I had picked out *Eleven Minutes*. Soon, my arms were full of books. He stacked them as if I had all the strength of Atlas. I didn't.

While I read the back of the books, the man adjusted a few spines and then noticed a stack in disarray.

"These damn housewives..." he said, picking up the books and organizing each one under the subject, "Philosophy and Self-Help." "They come in here crying because so and so died or their husband cheated on them, or their kid hates them. I mean, please. The nerve!"

I gave him a slight smile.

"Well, what books do they typically read when that stuff happens?" I asked. He seemed embarrassed at his outburst after he realized I wasn't kidding around.

"Oh, ok, well those really aren't my thing, I live here in the real world..." he said. "But if you need ideas, here are my top sellers in this category."

As I took each one and stacked it in with the novels, the cynical man rallied to help me chart my spiritual awakening. I soon had a range of books from every culture, giving me hope that somewhere deep in those books, I could find a way out of myself. The one on interpreting dreams made me optimistic that my recent vision about Ms. Mendoza could be a sign instead of a nightmare.

He retrieved two wimpy looking plastic bags from under his counter. He split the books between the bags.

"This should work, all you have to do is stay balanced," he said. "You will make the trip with no trouble."

I handed him about one-hundred-and-sixty dollars' worth of currency. I saw the first smile from him since I arrived. Yes, I was a tourist, and now I had plenty to read. No strength training today. The lingering street smell hit my nose when I stepped down from the store and started my trek back to the salon. For such a beautiful location, Valparaiso didn't fit my idea of a city I would call home for the rest of my life.

There were few cities I would ever enjoy calling home. Miami was one of them. I hadn't known how good I had it there in my chonga days.

As I walked, I passed a couple of older men eating sandwiches at a local deli.

Onions, pork and vegetables mixed in with all the other scents.

I called Charles when I arrived at the salon, and, after a half hour, he pulled up in front of the store to pick me up. Paco followed me out to the car and helped me with my many bags.

Once I was inside the car, Charles rolled down the window to greet his friend.

"Hello, mister, you want to give me a ride back to your house, weon?" Paco said.

"You wish," he said. "And it's not my house. You know that."

"Sure, Charles."

"Thanks for taking care of my girlfriend here," he said, as he looked over my new style.

Though I'd sweated out all the water I drank the day before, the flush on my skin gave me an extra boost of confidence alongside my hair.

"No problem. Your new style will go great with your boots, bella," he said, as he winked and waved as Charles pulled away from the curb.

"What does weon mean?" I asked. Charles laughed.

"Either jerk or amigo, take your pick," he said.

"I choose both for you."

With the car air conditioner blowing in his face, I doubted Charles emitted a drop of sweat in the Chilean sun. While we sat waiting in traffic, the cable cars racing past us, I looked outside the window and thought of the city, with its whole other way of speaking, talking, living the language I grew up with. Another round of dialects and my brain would be totally fried. I wasn't sure I would stay long enough to break in my new boots or read half the books I just bought. Change, change, change.

Chapter Seventeen

CHARLES LEFT ME HOME ALONE FOR TWO DAYS. WITH A LARGE, empty space, all mine, I walked around the house in my underwear and read my book on the terrace. *Eleven Minutes* was about a girl whose life that was almost as fucked up as mine. I tanned while enjoying the occasional breeze blowing in from the nearby harbor.

The house gym equipment was a serious workout aficionado's dream. Only the best for these two boys. I opened all the doors to let the air in and turned on the CD already in the player, a mixed Madonna album set to a techno beat. It fit my frenzied circuit training perfectly. I enjoyed the variety in what the iconic performer sang about as I lifted my legs to tone hips and thighs.

I jumped rope in between weight machines to get my heart rate up. With the beat prodding me through the speakers, an hour and a half flew by. A healthy sweat.

The more I progressed back to my old routines, the more emotions bubbled up, churning in my stomach. It wasn't the workout because it hurt in a good way. It was the gnawing feeling that I'd started a crazy cycle of training to kill all over again. Could I really go back to professional hits for a country I wasn't even a current citizen of? It never bothered me much when I was trying to escape my life as Chapa, but I was ready to move on to a new way of living.

I hadn't even lasted for a year and a half as one of the few female CIA assassins. Though I was drenched in my mini shorts and sports bra, I started to repeat the steps I practiced in Ms. Mendoza's ballroom studio. The beat was all wrong, but I kept dancing. My body shook, freely moving all by myself in an elegant way. I wondered what Ms. Mendoza's friends would do with the dance studio. Would they continue to gather and practice the ballroom routines? I wasn't strong enough to return and face them. A funeral appearance would open more questions to my involvement. I had come to the villa like an invisible guest, and I had left that way. Running away was the only way I could survive the pain of my current situation. That on top of what happened with Gabriel—the open wound was just too fragile to revisit.

After my rhapsodic sweat session, I sat on the bed and opened the folders. Why were my life changes always summarized in a folder marked "Classified"? The folder world was intense.

The documents were out of order, as if someone printed them from different sources. Thank you, Charles. He always delivered.

I read a summary of the file labeled, "The Dirty War." I had some background on the legacy of CIA work in Latin America, but the Argentinian government was responsible for the disappearance or killing of between 10,000 and 30,000 of its own citizens. Between 1976 and 1983, the CIA was actively working in Argentina to gather information and witness a massacre unfolding in real time.

The first document was from the National Security Council, March 25, 1984, and contained intelligence that "two retired army generals have a plan to pressure and ultimately remove the government of President Raul Alfonsin." In black margin marker, someone had written on the copy, "Argentine Military, Dirty War."

My father wrote the report. As I read through the eleven-point plan the generals crafted, I was reminded how all these tactics were so typical. This report was put together after I was born. He was still active while I was a toddler. It was the last paragraph about the coup that explained how the generals planned to bomb Alfonsin and human rights groups as "anti-military targets."

Another document recorded a conversation between U.S. Congressman Stephen Solarz and the Colombian president, with Solarz explaining why killing anti-government leftists was immoral and unjustified. He asked,

"What can a country do to protect itself against massive guerilla terrorism?"

The Colombian president, Bettancur, had replied, "There had been no will on the part of the Argentine authorities to correct abuses. They had not thought for human dignity. There was no justice. The Argentine Government had been an absolutist system enmeshed in its own authoritarian idolatry which was unable to cope with its own serious problem."

The transcript was recorded and translated by my mother a year after I was born. Three hours later, I was thoroughly shocked, upset, and at the same time impressed by what I read.

A full conversation between the Solarz and Fidel Castro took an hour to read, and was about the global governments and the machinations of politics and war. My mom was listening to it.

Even as I learned about my parents' work, I stopped searching for the reason they left me alone. As twenty-somethings, they were in the thick of something bigger than me. Bigger than our family.

I considered the soldier parents who deployed with me in Iraq. They built a life. They created a family. And then they walked away from it. A mission, a duty, a sacrifice. I thought again about the crying mother. She kept coming back to me. After leaving her eight-month-old baby boy to serve a year away. She cried every time she tried to connect with him on the staticky webcam, her husband inept at holding a baby and working the technology. When she came back, she told me her son wouldn't let her hold him. He didn't know who she was anymore.

I was much older than that baby boy when my parents chose country over family. By their example, and unencumbered by them, I was reincarnated as their true daughter, attaching myself to men as quickly as they became useful to my cause. And after everything, I didn't need parents. I needed what any soldier needs—to be useful, to be valuable and to have a purpose. My name wasn't even Concepcion Chapa anymore, it was whatever identity was issued to me. Always ready.

I picked up the first book about reincarnation. I couldn't put it down. Tears flowed effortlessly as I soaked up the ideas. The ideas that millions of people believed across the world, a timeless connection of everything as one and the many cycles of the soul, resonated deep within me. I wasn't one life, and the things I did were part of the lessons I had to learn in this lifetime. I had to find a way to forgive myself and turn the page.

When Charles returned home, I had showered and wiped the crazy off my face. I acted a little less like a needy houseguest after I cleaned the first and third floors from top to bottom. There were no skeletons in the walk-in closets, an unusual feature for a

European-style house, but I had gotten my first glimpse of Sergio in one of the many drawers I rifled through. It was a photograph of him and a beautiful brunette, hugging one another tightly and smiling. A sister, close friend perhaps? I had yet to find a photo of Charles, but he was sensitive about his personal space.

Sergio was handsome and metro-masculine like Charles. Not exactly what I expected when I thought of a gay artist. But wasn't I just full of stereotypes way off the mark? I banked on men and women underestimating me. It was the clear advantage I had over the other sex. Gabriel looked like what he was, a killer. Until someone saw the gun in my hand, they didn't have a clue I was there to end their life.

I told Charles I couldn't do a job where any amount of torture was involved because I didn't have it in me anymore. I was a finisher. If I came knocking at the door it wasn't for information. Strangely, I considered the interrogators the real bastards of the agency, sick and ruthless. Some of them were ruined after doing an assassin's work. Many of them never actually killed any of their victims. Gabriel couldn't understand my logic about torture because, in his mind, torture yielded the best information.

"I brought you a little something," Charles said. He came to meet me on the terrace where I was reading and rereading the pages of my book about interpreting dreams. He handed me my laptop, a piece of my life that survived the fire. I could have easily bought another one, but it seemed to make Charles happy that he had rescued something for me.

"Thank you, Charles," I said, taking the thin grey computer into my hands. "Now I don't have to spend money on a new one." I tried to sound sincere, but the words came out with the opposite meaning.

"Oh, love, I am feeling how much you appreciate it. But it was of no consequence to me. I just didn't want it ending up in any other grubby hands. Who knows what sort of tawdry sex video you have stored on the hard drive?"

"In that case your efforts are much appreciated," I said, in a rather sarcastic manner. "But, in all honesty any sex videos I ever starred in are stored on your surveillance footage."

He lightly kicked my leg while I was seated on the swinging bench, with my recovered laptop resting on my knees. I had the effect I hoped for. He had turned a bit red, but it was meant as a joke.

"I'm just kidding. It comes with the territory. I'm aware."

"But besides that, I loaded a program on the desktop. A little something our large brain individuals at NSA gave us."

The National Security Agency was always schooling the CIA on the finer points of secrecy.

"No rush, but when you want to, start your search for what comes next for you," Charles said. "Give it a whirl."

Whirling anything on the computer sounded fun but deciding my future assignment didn't seem like an easy, breezy task. Part of me wanted to start looking, but it had not even been a week since the fire.

"Did you get any information on the funeral arrangements for my friend?" I asked before he reached the open door to the kitchen.

"Nothing concrete, but it seems that one of her many admirers from the dance studio, a Mr. De Lula, was taking over the whole deal," he said. "Your previous home will be renovated and kept inside the agency. It's a great location, and, despite what happened there, there wasn't much we couldn't do. The neighbors live very private lives, unfortunately for your friend but fortunately for us. Who's to say what other relatives will come and claim the property after it is fixed up?"

It all sounded perfectly reasonable, and that made me uncomfortable. Was I disposable? If I would have died but left the home intact, would someone else be in my bed? Yes. I would just have to get over it if Charles was the practical, typical man of the operation. I couldn't ever deny my feelings, but I didn't have to show them to someone incapable of seeing it from my point of view. We were in a very dangerous business.

"Charles, if you don't mind, I think I will stay here a little while before I make any important decisions." A practical answer, and he nodded in agreement.

"What's that book you are reading?" he asked. "Interpreting dreams, are we?"

I closed the cover. "I'm trying to figure out how to sleep better at night. I really lost myself this last time. Death didn't feel that far away for me."

He furrowed his brow, "I know. You were a puddle when I found you. It's important to have something to believe in. Something just for you. No agency or brain-washing training stuff."

"Well, I decided I'm part of a larger universe," I said, twirling my hair and looking out into the horizon. "I'm going to come back as a Komodo dragon with all the horrible stuff I've done in this lifetime."

"Oh, darling. Don't be so sure that's not an upgrade. Being human is really hard. And you've had a hard life."

I closed my eyes. My thoughts were spinning with all the new information I had to sift through. Charles was the coach I needed.

"Yes, but I'm done with all the fear and self-loathing. I learned I can grow, I can change and it really isn't all about me."

"Oh, but it is," Charles said. "Just don't join a cult or anything with whatever it is you are reading."

I laughed. "Cults are for followers. I'm unlocking the God particle within myself, thank you very much. And for what it's worth, the housewives who buy all these books are the real heroes."

"Well, I will leave you to it." he said, lightly touching my shoulder as he passed. "Keep going, dear girl. I'm proud of you."

After six weeks of sweating off fifteen pounds and flying through all my bookstore purchases, I was settling into my new apartment. It was considerably smaller than my Italian style villa and less desirable to decorate but I had to keep up appearances. It was a true testament to the new and possibly improved outlook I had on my life. I asked to be sent to the most meaningless appointment where I could not possibly fuck anything up, or anyone else for that matter. I lived on the outskirts of Camp Bondsteel, a U.S. military camp in Kosovo.

The new location was so far removed from my last occupation that I barely had any work to fill up my day. In all honesty, I felt incredibly greedy with all this free time. On paper, I was a liaison to the United States military from the Argentinian military, but I ran a secret CIA prison on the compound. I maintained the personnel and the paperwork on the off chance the U.S. had someone to put inside. It hadn't held a single prisoner since it was built in the year 2001.

I relaxed in one of the cells and read my latest purchase from the Post Exchange, and I couldn't help but think of Charles. He turned out to be a good friend after all. How did he find this post? It hadn't even been listed on the master list he loaded onto my computer. He made a couple calls when I refused all the locations listed. I wanted something in Europe because Africa was full of impossible targets that could very well take my life, as the warlords and gangsters had taken many other agents' lives. Asia carried the risk of running into Gabriel, and I wanted to get out of South America.

Eastern Europe didn't register to me as a place where we would be operating. The country didn't have anything the United States usually went to war over. No oil, no coveted natural resources, and no inability to form an enemy coalition against us. But here I was. Living the life of self-discovery after a career of working the hard cases. I was what I hated as a young soldier. I was tired of all the gung-ho, hooah jobs, and I wanted to get off the kill circuit. I couldn't go back to any of my old lives. I couldn't have a completely normal one either, but I could serve my country out of the line of fire.

My assigned military police officer rattled on the bar to alert me that he was taking over. It could be called guard duty, like I pulled in Iraq, but we didn't have anyone to guard.

Private First Class Kevich knew not to ask too many questions. He was a quiet but efficient young man. Nowhere near the kind of soldier I was. I didn't hold it against him that his only experience was this summer camp instead of Iraq or

Afghanistan. If I was honest with myself, I shouldn't wish him any combat experience. I kept my mouth shut. He didn't ask why an Argentinian was guarding this place or why I gave out his orders. He thought I was hot, but I wasn't going to go there with anyone here. This was just a meatsuit that helped me along the way.

If I engaged with him, it might ruin a good thing for me. It would be more complicated if we received a prisoner to guard, so I just crossed my fingers and hoped for the best.

"See you tomorrow, Kevich."

"Yeah, tomorrow," he answered, probably already checking his Facebook status on our computer system as I was walking out. He needed to learn not to save his account passwords on our shared computer.

I stepped on to the gravel-paved path and found my Mitsubishi Montero Sport. It came with the assignment, and it was a perfect fit for the iffy road system surrounding the camp. I passed through the gates and the civilian security guard waved me through. Most of the guys and a few of the women were former military, but they made more money going the civilian contractor route. It was quieter when I left than when I came in. Many of the local workers had already left for the day. Both Kosovo Albanians and Kosovo Serbians made their living at the camp. Our camp, along with several others, employed thousands of people in a country with one of the highest un-employment rates, but it had been worse.

I picked up speed on roads named after animals, like Hawk Road and Lion Road. I did not want to get rear-ended by any crazy drivers. Motor vehicle accidents were the most common and easiest way to die in this country, besides pissing me off.

We should make soldiers direct traffic and the mission would probably have a bigger impact. Hearts and minds, how about traffics rules and civilized road manners? The camp had only a thousand or so soldiers from various Guard and Reserve units, but there were still quite a few U.S. citizens who worked as support staff. I passed through the town of Ferizaj to get on the highway. I was going to the capitol, Pristina, about an hour away for dance class. I technically wore a uniform that fit in better in Pristina than on the American camp.

I liked being around my fellow countrymen, but for now I wasn't ready to interact with the soldiers. It was a little closer to home but a little too risky as well. They could go home; this was my home. While the soldiers put their relationships and careers on hold for a year of duty, it wasn't the same for me. I would stay if they would let me. Pristina was one of the bigger cities where I could interact with international police, ambassadors, diplomats, and aid workers and be welcomed no matter what. I began attending some of the UN police functions because technically that was where my uniform came from.

A dance class was the best thing to do on a Thursday night at the UNMIK building. I didn't need the lessons, but after reading in a cell all day, it felt good to be around other people.

Movement was medicine to me, and every time I put on my dancing shoes, I thought of my favorite instructor, Ms. Mendoza. Her voice rang in my ears, the soft counting of the steps. Her passion kept me going. And I changed my attitude right around when I thought about her friendship and how important it was to me. By engaging with her memory, I kept the nightmare about her death at bay. She danced her life away, and I couldn't think of a better use of my time.

I showed my badge to another civilian police officer, a tall guy from The Netherlands. Weren't all Dutch people tall? This guy was a little too tall.

After I cleared security, I parked my SUV in the official business spot near the entrance. I still had on my black, fitted uniform and beret, matching the black vehicle. I had kept my shortened haircut from my time in Chile, but I did have it pulled back into a bun, with the aid of bobby pins. I put on some semblance of a professional appearance. I grabbed my backpack from the backseat and walked a short distance to the locker room.

"*Ciao, Sofia,*" a woman said. Only one woman called me by my first name.

"*Ciao, Katja! Bailamos.*"

The forty-something instructor greeted me. She had already changed her clothes. In addition to her work as a Swedish nurse, she taught salsa and ballet. I would have loved to try ballet, but the classiness overwhelmed me. That seemed more suited to Joelle's body type.

Fifteen minutes later, the class of men and women warmed up to the easy sequence Katja gave us. Floor length mirrors on all sides. The steps reverberated in my brain. I had to shut out the other students who either weren't serious, weren't capable, or both. I needed to dance for my own sanity. Within the first ten minutes, we were sweating, and I kept Katja in my sights. I had the feeling that a couple of men were checking out my ass, but Katja would home in on them sooner or later.

She moved so gracefully, though I didn't see the fire in her steps. Ms. Mendoza never missed a step like Katja did, but Katja was so full of life and heart, and that was important. Ms.

Mendoza, an experienced teacher, overemphasized her steps to keep us on the beat. I missed her most when I danced. After class, I waited until all the other students had left.

"Sofia, I am so glad you stayed," she said. "Want a coffee?"

"Coffee sounds just right," I said.

Getting a coffee was like having a cocktail in the States. The difference was that at two a.m., the bar was full of coffee drinkers, not boozy drunks.

We sat down at a table on the first floor of the UN press building. The café had everything any good European could want. Some patrons stood and downed their tiny shots of Italian espresso while others sat on overstuffed divans and sipped Turkish brewed cups. I preferred Italian.

"Thank you for inviting me," I said, after we ordered our drinks. Though I was used to getting attention, it seemed all eyes were on my teacher. A lesser woman might have been jealous.

"Thank you for meeting me," she said. "I like to get outside my usual circle of colleagues."

"Me too," I said, but who was I kidding? My only real colleague now was Charles. I answered to no one but him. That suited me fine. He was the only one who wanted me, after all.

The server brought out our respective drinks, hers a café au lait, and mine a macchiato. The taste wasn't quite authentic, but we were in Kosovo, not South America or Rome. She sipped her drink while I tested the espresso's temperature, finishing the cup in three mouthfuls.

The small café was packed with women and men both young and old, from all corners of the globe . It seemed like the oldest ones came from the United States. I'd overheard that they were the rejects or retirees of the police forces in the States.

I asked Charles and he explained that many of the men could cross the ocean and earn three times the salary. Their main activity seemed to be flirting with the local Kosovars and, in some cases, marrying them. Katja glanced over her coffee cup and her eyes settled upon a balding man with his hand wrapped around an eighteen-year-old local girl.

"The internationals here call this green card loving. It's too much for me to bear sometimes," Katja said. She spoke accented English very well, and I appreciated her joke.

"I don't know which one is worse off, the old American or the Kosovo Albanian. She looks like she could spend his money real fast."

Katja considered this and smiled.

"I like the way you think, Sofia," she paused. "I have an idea for you and it's purely selfish."

"And what's that?"

I had no idea what it could be. I barely knew the tall, blonde woman.

"You should teach the salsa class."

As soon as she said it, my eyebrows raised to their surgically enhanced high point. "Why would I do that? You're a great instructor."

"Consider it, at least," she said, and I realized she had thought about this seriously. "You have been to three of my classes and you can dance circles around the whole lot of us."

Could I? I wasn't paying attention to anyone else.

"Where did you learn the salsa?" she asked. I decided to give her most of the truth.

"I recently spent a lot of time learning ballroom dancing with a good friend of mine. I learned the cumbia which is similar,"

I said. "Salsa much earlier, when I was a teenager maybe, but I didn't have choreographed steps."

Dancing couldn't give away my identity.

"You are obviously much better than you think you are," she said. She finished her milky concoction. "You don't have to make a decision. It's just something to pass the time. The pay is something like fifty dollars. You can't buy anything with that, but it is nice to have someplace to dance."

She was right. If Katja didn't teach the class, I didn't know what I would have done with so much time.

"I'll think about it," I said. It was all I could offer at this point. "Will you teach another ballet class at the same time?"

"Nooo," she started to laugh, a girlish giggle. "I would come to your class. We could switch places. I could learn some of your routines like you've perfected mine."

"What if we could teach together? Then I would not feel like such a novice."

"That wouldn't work for me. You are in police. You understand it. There has to be a leader," she said. "Otherwise we would give all the horny men a heart attack with both of us telling them how to move."

"Like they need an excuse," I said, curling my mouth in a smile.

I checked my watch. It was getting late, but the combination of the espresso and the idea of teaching salsa made me loath to drive back to the base. Pristina was where all the fun things happened.

She shifted in her seat and I sensed she was also thinking about the time.

"I better get going." I stood and started to collect my things. I placed a small tip for the waiter on the table. I had to remember not to over tip. I was supposed to be South American, not from the land of overzealous tippers. "Thank you for the offer, Katja. I will give you a call at your office. Maybe we can get together again sometime."

"Yes, we will," she said. "I want you to teach me the paso double... I told you I was selfish."

"Oh, I see, the paso doble. Con seguridad. You like pushing me into the role of teacher." I smiled. In my heart, I was flattered. I hoped I made Ms. Mendoza feel the same way.

On the drive back to Ferizaj, I got stuck behind a green tractor that looked like it would have fit in better forty years ago.

The body was supplemented with parts from at least two other tractors. I was no expert, but the different colors tipped me off. Two young boys rode alongside their grandpa, one of them playing an old-fashioned Gameboy and the other on a cellphone. A juxtaposition of old versus new. I traveled from the cityscape to the countryside in less than an hour. I had no idea what Kosovar farmers actually grew, but I noticed tractors were a major source of transportation outside the city.

I was in the middle of something that brought over fifty countries together. Diplomacy in action or inaction depending on who I asked. I didn't have the feeling of death or despair here, and I thought about how different my life would have turned out if Joelle and I spent a year here instead of a combat zone. The soldiers carried weapons here, but it seemed more out of ceremony or due diligence than actual threat.

I reached my apartment at ten p.m., and the smell of garlic assaulted my senses as I climbed the staircase. This was apartment living: babies crying, kids playing, voices chatting away on cellphones, husbands yelling over the news hoping someone in the home would acknowledge their dominance. I lived so far from reality as a contract killer that it made my profession seem like it was the only thing that existed. I understood why Charles said it was better that I died in my former life than carry on as it was. I couldn't come back to my condo after I did "my duty." It must be the new protocol to create a force outside the United States with no ties back to it.

If I stayed in Miami, I would be lying to everyone I knew. By now, I'd talked myself into believing I'd just been reincarnated within the same lifetime. I searched out examples in history of people leading double-lives. I was a change agent, a chameleon. But my soul remained mine.

I sat on the plush sofa, turned on the television, and watched a Mexican soap opera on satellite. The tiny dishes dotted every apartment, looking like a disease on all the buildings.

I had tears in my eyes when I finally caught on to the storyline. I wasn't sure exactly what touched me about the drama or if internally I just needed a good cry. One thing I was sure about was that this life wasn't my own anymore. All these choices led me to giving more and more of myself but getting nothing in return. Where was my happy ending? Stolen and a world away. At least I had Charles. A tragedy of unrequited love, but it was something. I dried my eyes and went to check my email.

Chapter Eighteen

W HEN MY INBOX LOADED, I HAD AN ENCRYPTED FILE FROM NONE other than my favorite CIA handler. The subject line was "Bloody fucking hell." I almost laughed until I considered what it meant. Charles could have some bad news.

I checked my cell phone. I had forgotten to switch it over from silent after my dance class. Amateur mistake: I had three missed calls from an unknown number. I decided to check my email before calling Charles back. A few more minutes of not knowing wouldn't hurt.

I clicked on the email icon and waited for three photographs to load. The first photo was grainy. Joelle was having a coffee. Okay, fine. I hadn't expected any updates on her, but Charles knew she was part of my humanity and so maybe he wanted to keep me updated. The photo showed a pleasant little shop, European maybe. She was spending some of that money after all. The second picture had me saying, "Oh, fuck, Joelle!"

It wasn't at all controversial what she was doing. Actually, it was the same thing I was doing, checking her email on the computer. But it was where she was doing it that shocked me. The man in the foreground was most definitely a local Kosovar, and the sign read, "Internet café—Pristina."

Joelle was in Pristina. The timestamp was earlier today. The third photograph showed her walking in a nice neighborhood with another local.

While I was reading *The Pilgrimage*, Joelle had made her own journey to the exact location I was in.

I printed the photographs to examine the details later. The sounds from other apartments were minimal. I assumed the rest of the building had gone to bed. I called Charles and though I wanted to shout into the phone, I kept my voice to almost a whisper. The neighbors understood English.

"Charles, what happened? Why is she here?" I asked as soon as I heard his groggy voice.

"We are working on it. But we only found out last night."

"So, what do you know?" I asked. If I sounded aggravated, I wasn't. I was a little nervous and at the same time curious as to why she came to Kosovo. I hoped it was not because of me. No way to be sure unless I asked her.

"We were alerted three days ago by our Homeland Security Department," he said. "After I pulled surveillance on her, we put her on a watch list just to be safe. A GPS device in her luggage led us right to her. We are using some agents we had in Bulgaria now. We know she is alone, but she lives with others, a Kosovo-Albanian who is here on a student visit from the United States, and a Finnish student. It will take time to find out more. You now know what I know," he said.

"Okay, but it's not enough," I said, whispering, more out of shock than secrecy. "I can't believe she's here."

"I will ask you one time, and one time only, did you contact her in any way?" Charles asked, sounding deadly serious.

"Absolutely not."

I didn't elaborate because I couldn't explain something I wouldn't do, not to her, not to the agency, and not to myself either. I didn't want to rock the boat.

"Any chance Gianni Catanese or Chuey Valderron have a lead on me?"

"No, they have given up the search by all accounts. They believe something doesn't add up, but they don't know what, and that is the best we can do in many cases. They are law enforcement."

When Charles spoke, his Sussex accent, training or not, made everything sound like he was in control. It was smart to keep a tracker on Joelle McCoy because I could have run into her in Pristina at the coffee shop or gas station.

We weren't the same people anymore. I had undergone the most dramatic transformation, but I was also surprised to find Joelle outside of her comfortable Missouri existence.

"What should I do, Charles?" I asked. "I need you to tell me what to do next."

"I would stay as far away as possible," he said. "I have to remind you, you are not Concepcion Chapa anymore, not even a little bit. If she saw you on the street or in a café, she wouldn't recognize you."

My mind wandered. I still never exactly got an answer as to why I had to change my face, but this situation showed how important it was to keep my cover intact.

"A question, sir. Who were you, Charles, before you became a British-born gentleman?"

He changed his tone and gave me his best Russian accent, "I was a very Russian warrior."

"Really?"

I knew he was joking but maybe there was some truth to it.

"Before I was Russian, I was Australian, a little like Crocodile Dundee."

He was great with accents.

"Who can you be?" I asked. He tried out his Indian, American, and French accents on me. I would have believed any one of them if he had stayed with one of them consistently. He was too suave to be from the United States. He shuddered at all my nasty little habits.

"I don't want to leave here just yet," I said. "It suits me."

"No such thing, but I know what you mean. You are a very lucky girl.

"Are you sure you don't want any other contracts? We got a new one in Bolivia. Sick, sick individuals. You would enjoy helping them take a permanent vacation."

"I don't want that kind of work ever again. I want to do my job here," I said. "I sit in a prison cell all day. It's very Zen. I understand why everyone finds religion in prison."

"Good for you," he said. "If prison is your gig, Guantanamo always remains open."

"No, not until I've exhausted all other options," I said. "There are innocent people in there. I watched a documentary on it."

"Yeah, you're right, but we're stuck in a catch twenty-two there. On another note, you're being very good with the little Polish boy, too," he said. "No incidents yet."

"I can learn from my mistakes, Charles," I said. "I am capable of seeing the light. Last time I got involved with somebody, it was way worse than being alone ever was."

"You are wrong there. It is better to have loved."

"Charles," I said, "not today."

"Fine, I will call you if we get any more information. By the way, I didn't tell the home office anything directly about this. They would pull you out in three seconds flat."

"You got that right."

I went to sleep that night thinking of all the complex scenarios that could have brought Joelle McCoy to Kosovo. I didn't admit it to Charles, but I was genuinely happy she was here.

Despite some of the conspiracy theory scenarios, she was traveling again and spending her money.

She was living less than an hour away from here. She surely had surveillance on her by now.

I drifted off sometime in the early hours, before the light peeked into my room and I awoke to the Muslim call to prayer. I tried to fall back asleep but the best I could manage was to keep my eyes closed. The voice over the loudspeaker almost lulled me to sleep. Five, ten minutes passed, and I officially gave up trying. I threw my legs off the side of the bed and willed myself to get ready for the day.

I placed my Pilates mat close to the door so I could take it to the prison with me. I considered what would happen if someone in the government higher than Charles found my personnel file and decided to check on what one of the highest paid assassins was currently doing with her time.

"Um, yes, sir, Mr. Director. We do have an agent on prison detail. She is former Army, former FBI, and usually works for us now on contract eliminations. Currently, she reads books and does Pilates all day. Oh, and she's the daughter of our highest paid intelligence agents."

That would be some kind of report.

I decided I would accept Katja's offer to take over her class. At least I would stay in shape and, with my fifty-dollar paycheck, I could pay for the gas to get there. This job paid $75,000 a year. Considerably less than my $50,000 contracts for one job, but it could be worse.

I carefully dressed in one of several uniforms hanging in my closet. Like a good soldier, I polished the tips of my black boots to a mirror finish.

I stopped to pick up breakfast from one of the two dining facilities. It was one of my rare interactions with the U.S. soldiers on the camp.

The food was bland but good, considering they had to feed something like a thousand people. Fresh fruit and cow's milk were flown in from Germany every few days on C-130s. The Pentagon did it to make us all feel at home and in order to employ only certain government contractors.

Many of the taxpayers didn't eat as well as we did, but the military was the sacred cow regarding funding. I smiled at that thought. I didn't want to start the day out being cynical, but I felt a bit of a stinging feeling when I thought of how easy some soldiers had it compared to others around the world. Could Joelle be here to work with the United States in some capacity?

I doubted it, but only time would tell. I tapped Kevich on the shoulder. He awoke without a fuss. His assignment was a twelve-hour overnight shift during which after he cleaned the cells and did some minimal paperwork, and could wake up to a smiling boss who never said a word about him sleeping on the job. If I had been his sergeant during my Army days, I would have smoked the shit out of him, made him do overhead arm claps and plié' girlie squads until his legs and arms fell off. No pushups, though, because guys liked pushups; only ballerina moves. Arm lifts were embarrassing.

But I wasn't his sergeant and I didn't have to follow the rules. I knew by now that life was too short. I had a Hakuna-Matata attitude. It meant no worries.

Chapter Nineteen

"CHARLES, I AM GOING TO TEACH A SALSA CLASS IN PRISTINA."

"Um, okay... And why would you do that?"

"Because I want to, and life is short and all that stuff. Any rules about that?"

"Of course, there aren't. We can consider it deep cover. You certainly studied enough with your late friend to teach any dance."

"I was just checking," I said, delaying my real request until the tail end of the conversation. "Oh, and Charles... What is Gabriel's number?"

"Are you sure you want to know?" he asked.

"No, but give it to me anyways, and please don't listen in if you have a choice."

"He is working in the northern part of Laos. You should be able to reach him on his satellite phone I think," he said. "I have to tell you that I am not his handler anymore."

He rattled off the many numbers.

I wrote them on the back of a napkin. I heard Charles take a deep breath.

"Concepcion, Sofia, whoever you are, I have to tell you something before you make that call," he said.

"Whatever it is, Charles, don't talk me out of this," I said, certain he would try.

"Okay, then," he said, and hung up.

I drove back to my apartment in Ferizaj and decided against going inside where the walls were paper-thin. What I had to say was private and I wanted to call Gabriel. I needed complete closure and to apologize.

He didn't answer. I left it at that. I wanted to make amends and move on, be the best version of myself I could be.

I began teaching salsa the following week and decided before class I would introduce myself to the students at the door.

I heard names from across the globe from the eclectic group of students. There was an Adelaide, a Francesco, a Gunther, Fatima, Paul, Jackie, and a Joelle.

Smiling weakly at the latest student to grip my hand and pass on through, I couldn't remember who else came through the door. I was stunned. I wanted to run away or hug her all at the same time. I was being tested like never before. Joelle McCoy was Sofia Paltrini's salsa student.

What could I do? Run out? Of course, I could, but how would this look to Charles? Could I handle it? Tensed up and on autopilot, I taught the routine from memory, and more than a few times I caught myself watching my battle buddy while she was staring at her feet. She had to work on her confidence.

After we finished, I heard her say thanks before she exited with her roommate, the local girl from the photos.

I barely slept that night. I couldn't explain it to Charles when he called about the first class.

He asked about Gabriel instead, and I didn't want to go into it with him. He already had too much control over my life. He knew without a doubt that she was dancing in my class, and her surveillance team could very well have be in there, too. We do come in all shapes and sizes, trained to blend in.

The next day I met a couple of women from the UNMIK building, Sgt. Castillo and Alma, for a coffee. They were both Argentinian soldiers. I joined the women at the Italian café at the end of a strip of small shops and restaurants. I wanted to see how they were getting along and especially how Alma was doing. I was serving as her witness. Alma was suffering from PTSD after a local boy died in a landmine explosion while she was on patrol in the area .

As to be expected, Sgt. Castillo, her leader, greeted me warmly, but Alma was another story. I saw the wheels turning behind her eyes. She wasn't doing well.

"Do you miss home?" I asked, testing the waters with an easy question.

"I think I will be leaving in a month or so," she answered.

The thought of being in Argentina no doubt comforted her.

I had heard from Sgt. Castillo that the death of the local boy was ruled an accident.

Alma had a heavy burden to bear. It wasn't her fault, but being that close to death was too much in the internationally charged environment of Kosovo. Sgt. Castillo broached the subject of my salsa class. Apparently, someone name Armando told her I was an excellent instructor who had "a fire in her belly for dance."

"Will you stay in the military when you return to Argentina?" I asked. The question was meant to be harmless, but my tone rang false to my ears.

Sgt. Castillo turned to hear Alma's response. It was a question she, too, had been forced to answer during her career.

Alma looked at me with sad eyes and shrugged her thin frame in response.

"And, do what? This is what I know," she said. "There are not as many opportunities as you think for me in Argentina. My whole family are ranchers, and I wanted to get away from the life. It's a good one but it isn't for me."

It didn't sound like an insult, more like a fact.

"You can do other things," I said, quietly. "There is always a choice."

This was the extent of my advice on the subject. It wasn't right to insert myself completely.

The Argentinian government would let her stay in the military with PTSD, just as my own kept me in its service. We were a new breed of soldiers with a lot of money invested in our military futures.

Later that night, I went to the Internet café and paid for information on Joelle. All I needed was her new email address.

The man at the front desk scrolled through a lengthy Excel file on his computer, and I had the email in my hands within a matter of minutes. The CIA wasn't the only one keeping tabs on people. The local population were gathering information about internationals even as they served our needs. It was common sense in a country that didn't exist a year ago.

I sat down and created a fake email account and decided to write to my friend. I had to heal from the inside out, and making myself a bit more honest was a great way to start. I'd trained to lie without detection, but it was being honest, after so much deceit, that I considered the boldest of moves.

I couldn't come right out and tell her who I was, for my own security. I didn't want to scare her. She couldn't know my new identity or who I worked for, but she needed to become more aware of her surroundings. I could alleviate any of her remaining grief and uncertainty about my death.

Even after closing the browser and deleting the program's cache, I doubted I had complete secrecy, but the message would only make sense to its recipient.

I was almost out the door.

"Please come again," the man at the desk said.

Once outside, I waited a few minutes before turning in the direction of my vehicle. After what I just wrote, I had nothing to lose except my life.

Joelle would receive my email and know I walked these streets. I was done lying to my best friend, and I had to put her mind at ease. The fact that she was out of the United States meant it would be much easier for someone to kill her and get away with it. It happened every day.

I opened the driver's side door to my vehicle. Something was wrong. A small click. A red rose on my seat. The parking lot was empty, but the streets were still busy.

I bit my lip, stepped away, and started running. I felt pinpricks of heat on my skin. The explosion burned behind me as I fell forward with the force of the blast. A woman screamed, broken, in pain. It was me. Ms. Mendoza all over again.

"Help," the words barely escaped my lips. "Help..." The words flowed on repeat, a refrain I couldn't control.

What a cowardly way to try to kill me.

The puffy clouds were on parade, and as I looked up at the sky, a large patch of them moved, as if to show me something was going to change. Was this the way I was supposed to die? After so many careful moves, I had made a mistake and underestimated someone.

Me, as the bringer of so much pain and death. I was no longer playing god. Why did I have to die? After all, I was reborn in that fire. Staying here would mean more questions and more authorities around whom I may not be able to hold myself.

Who tried to kill me? Charles was elusive and cryptic, but my instincts made me comfortable with him. The idea of him trying to kill me was too much to bear. After Ms. Mendoza's death, he had every right to end my life. I could have exposed his cover with my babbling.

I dialed his number, but the phone was shut off. His phone was never off, ever.

I picked myself up and walked to a taxi.

"Ferizaj, please," I said to the driver. He smiled, a few rotten teeth still hanging in the front of his mouth.

"Of course, Madame," he said, happy with the astronomical fare he was going to charge me for the long drive. "We'll be there in no time."

Chapter Twenty

I WAS PASSED OUT IN MY FERIZAJ APARTMENT WITH THE TELEVI-sion on in the background when I heard a knock at the door. The adrenaline from the bombing knocked me out cold as soon as I was out of harm's way. A concussion, maybe?

My senses heightened, and I rolled off the couch to the ground. After a few minutes passed with no one shooting through the door, I low crawled to the kitchen area, hoping my visitor wouldn't hear me moving.

"Open the door, Sofia," a low voice said. "It's Charles. I heard what happened, and I am not here to finish you off."

So, he knew I suspected him. Who else knew me better than Charles? No one did, not even Joelle.

I stood up and straightened my black T-shirt and pants then grabbed my weapon off the counter.

"I'm opening the door slowly, but no sudden movements," I yelled into the door.

"I hear you, and I'm not moving until you say so," he said. "I was on a plane when it happened. I thought I'd lost you."

I opened the door to Charles. His eyes were bloodshot and the scruff forming on his chin meant he hadn't shaved. He still looked better than I did after the explosion.

"Come in," I said, opening the door wide. "They haven't killed me yet."

"I see that," he stepped into the apartment and carefully closed the door behind him.

I walked to the couch and felt his arms around me, hugging me close.

"Oh, Charles, that's sweet," I said. "You actually care—"

His mouth met mine. He kissed my lips while his hands pulled me into him.

I tried to speak and move away, but he was stronger than I thought.

Where had this come from?

I mentally flashed through everything I knew about Charles and tried to conjure an image of him with a man in a compromising position. I thought of Sergio, but conveniently I had never actually met him. Paco could just be a friend—Charles would appeal to everyone even as a friend.

I finally pulled myself away.

"Charles, what's this, do you have me confused with a man?" I asked.

After I nearly died, it struck me as preposterous that this was the first question I asked. Not about who tried to kill me, but about his sexuality.

"My name is not Charles," he said. "No, I don't just like men. I like who I like, it's not about gender."

"Seriously, bisexual?" I said, pushing him away from me, hard. "You lied to me."

"I am your handler," he said. "Not your buddy. If I told you, it would have been awkward. You know you would have tried. It's not possible. So, I told a little lie. Our whole lives are about lies. I just can't keep hiding it from you anymore. Not when you almost died."

"Why did you have to lie?" I said, trying to focus on this new revelation. "We could have been good together."

"It wasn't possible," he said. "I had to put an action plan in writing about how I would handle the rogue FBI agent. Being your boyfriend wasn't part of the bargain. That was a deal-breaker if I wanted to be your handler."

"Then why now, Charles?" I asked. "I almost died today and now you're telling me that the only real thing about the past couple years was a charade. What were you waiting for?"

He sat on the couch, and I watched as he ran his hands through his hair. He was anxious. The calm and collected Charles was cracking.

"I was waiting for you to notice the way I looked at you, the way I cared for you, but most of all I was waiting to get over you," he said. "It hasn't happened yet. No matter how far away you go. I could tell you needed a friend and not a lover. You're also a trained killer so there's always a risk if you didn't like me. I..."

"Who tried to kill me?" I asked. Interrupting. "If it wasn't you, then who in the agency wants me dead?"

"We traced a wire transfer to a local Iranian bomb maker back to Aquila," he said. "He's under investigation, and he's trying to clean up any loose ends. The team your parents run stopped paying Aquila for your protection months ago. He was left high and dry with a cocaine problem, Sofia. He hated that. He turned on your parents because he wasn't good enough to join them. I think he wanted to kill you to draw them out. And he may have convinced Joelle to come here if that didn't work. How did she get here, of all places? The only person connecting both of you is him. She is your Achilles heel. The only tie back to your identity that matters."

"Aquila? Really! It wouldn't be the first time he fucked me over," I said. "Back to what you said before, what if I don't like you back, Charles?" I asked, testing his affection. "Where do we go from here?"

"Then I would say you are not being honest with yourself, and I don't blame you," he said. "Honesty is not our go-to policy."

I reached out for his hand and kissed it.

"Is this why you were always surveilling me?" I asked. "You must have a very high tolerance for jealousy, Charles. But why Gabriel then?"

"That was a mistake. I admit. That guy was trying to make a name for himself and writing in his reports about how unprofessional you were to work with. So the surveillance wasn't just one-sided. I had to prove he was lying about you. You have no idea," he said, shaking his head. "That was a really sad way to be close to you. I didn't want to feel this way. I tried not to. My career has been everything to me for so long and it meant trusting someone for the first time in my life."

"I won't tell, Charles," I said. "We can keep whatever this is a secret. I can't like or love anyone right now. I feel something for you, but I don't know if that's enough. I'm still trying to find a way to love myself."

"It must be jetlag, but I am not in the mood for keeping secrets any longer," he said.

He moved closer to me.

"I'm not that easy, Charles," I said. "I need to think about the idea of us for a while."

He saw in my eyes it wasn't going to happen between us so quickly. All the Eastern philosophy I studied was whispering to my inner voice, "Stay strong and do not go with the first person to show you affection."

"That's not the way this is supposed to go," he said. "I thought you would let me tear your clothes off once I kissed you. I dreamt of you for so long I need a shower to cool off. It was a long flight."

"Yes, and everything I know about everyone is a lie," I said. "So, excuse me, but I almost died. Fuck you and the kiss too."

It had been one hell of a kiss. But what had the past year taught me about myself? I was almost killed by a father-figure today, and my usually off-limits handler was throwing himself at me. It was too much for one day.

I watched as Charles walked away and released my hand. How had he imagined this would go? I was always left alone to pick up the pieces once a man fucked me over. Who was I to say that Charles would be different? He was the only constant in my life after Joelle. My friend when I had no one else. He handpicked Gabriel for me just to make me happy and then covered up the whole mess. He could have kicked me out of the agency a hundred times after so many mistakes.

The fact he was in love with me made it all make sense. His motives were now clear. He had hidden his own identity complete with a boyfriend as cover, though he had said he like both boys and girls. His preference was the person and not the gender. Was this why I felt his gaze on me in so many important moments?

I heard the shower turn on and thought about a naked Charles stepping in my dilapidated tub, probably using my favorite coconut body scrub.

I walked to the open bathroom door and watched his silhouette through the opaque shower curtain for a few seconds. I swallowed hard.

Pulling back the curtain, I looked at Charles in all his glory. His eyes met mine and I knew I was in trouble.

"Don't run from me, honey," he said, the soap running down his muscled abdomen. "I will always find you. You can have all of this as long as you are honest with me, just like before. I have seen how you lied to others and yourself. I need all of you, Concepcion Sofia Chapa Paltrini."

"Fine," I said. "But I haven't even got to try you out first. What if you're terrible in bed?"

"We're not in a bed if you haven't noticed," he said. "I am not going to dignify it with a response because you obviously haven't seen how crazy I am about you. Nothing about it can be terrible."

I left the bathroom and shut the door behind me. I was so frazzled from the bomb. I didn't trust my own feet on the ground quite yet.

I sat on the couch and tried to think about anything other than the man in my shower. I picked up the card deck of inspirational quotes that had gotten me through so many other situations. After shuffling for a minute, I picked out one from the Mexican author Don Miguel Ruiz: "Death is not the biggest fear we have; our biggest fear is taking the risk to be alive—the risk to be alive and express what we really are."

I had lived four lives, and at such a young age. Many people never lived outside their hometown because it was easier to be comfortable. I wasn't sure I should jump into the bed of my handler and ride off into the sunset. I was scared, and didn't know who I could go to for help.

A phone buzzed on the chair. It wasn't mine. Charles came out of the shower with my purple cotton towel wrapped around his waist. He nodded as I handed him his phone.

"This is Charles," he said. He spoke for a few minutes and hung up abruptly.

He turned to me, his face full of concern. "We have to go."

"Why?"

"It's not safe."

"I know that, but I thought you came here because it was—"

"Not anymore. Someone hit the van Joelle was in and she's in the hospital. She's okay though."

"Joelle, so he really targeted her?"

"Do you know who your weaknesses are? You are a walking liability with her," He was talking fast as he started to dress in front of me.

"I need to see her. I don't care anymore. I'm done with whatever this is but I'm going to see her at least one more time. I have nothing left, I have no one left."

The tears streamed down my face. The death, the accidents, the deceptions were too much for me. I couldn't take anymore. I wasn't strong enough.

Charles hugged me, his body still warm and wet from the shower. His hair dripped on me.

"You have me, you have me," he said.

"It's not enough," I said. "I'm done. Take me to see my friend."

Chapter Twenty-One

I WALKED OUT OF THE CAMP BONDSTEEL HOSPITAL AFTER SEEING Joelle into a bright sunny afternoon. She was going home and was going to be safe. In those stolen, private moments where I revealed my identity, our relationship was renewed.

"I've got your back, Jo," I whispered, as I left her once again, knowing I had to keep her alive and well. Her happiness was my happiness.

I promised her I would make sure she was safe. Walking the distance to my station at the prison, I needed to collect my things. Charles wanted to wait for me there.

Joelle made me feel better. I had choices. I could choose differently. She made me want to choose something other than service and sacrifice. What I had given was enough. My service was enough. I would take this face of a stranger and try to piece together what a life should be, with more Ms. Mendoza moments and more relationships built on something stronger than convenience. Concepcion Chapa was a formidable woman who used her power for good. Sofia Paltrini had lost so many of the best parts of Concepcion along the way.

As I entered the prison, Kovach tried to make his exit, patting me on the back.

"I hear you are headed home today," he said. "Nice to work with you."

I nodded and lightly touched his shoulder. I guess Charles was in charge now, telling everyone my business.

"Thank you for being a good partner, Kovach." He hesitated at the door and nodded.

Charles was waiting for me just inside, sitting at the metal desk that scraped my leg every time I stood up. I hated that old thing. "Look who came to visit."

I tracked his gaze to the prison cell. Aquila was sitting in one of them, looking pathetic in an old suit. A camouflaged man and a woman sat together in the other cell.

"That was fast," I said to Charles. "I didn't think you would take care of it right away." I was impressed with my handler.

"Oh love, it wasn't just me," he pointed to the couple.

I was confused. "Then why are they in a cell? Are they agency?"

"Kind of," Kovach said. "They followed me in here and asked if I had the keys. I took them off your desk, pulled my weapon, and they were willingly caged up together. I don't trust anyone." Kovach was clearly proud of his adventure.

Charles interrupted, "I had to separate them after the man almost killed our suspect. We need to get a little more info out of Aquila before the show is over."

I went over to Aquila and spit on the ground. "Fuck you! Fine about me but why Joelle?"

"Why not?" he said. "You can go thank your parents for hanging me out to dry. They are duplicitous scum and loyalty means nothing to them."

I ran to the other cell. The man stood up, but the woman looked down. Dark hair, light eyes, strong, average height. My father was a good-looking man.

"Concepcion..." the man said.

His voice, his husky, accented voice that had sung me to sleep as a kid and comforted me when I doubted myself.

I turned to her. She was still breathtaking, Charles was wrong. His standard of beauty wasn't mine. She was exotic with no makeup, lines showing her age, but with kind eyes.

They were my parents, but they were not my family.

"Concepcion...can you ask your friend here to let us out? We came here to rescue you. We got him, and we won't let him hurt you anymore."

I watched them but couldn't respond. My body numbed and I shuddered. That life was so long ago. The one with the family. Conflicting emotions flooded over me, but I couldn't let my parents hurt me anymore. I had people who loved me, who chose me, who searched for me and who wanted nothing in return. Mothers and fathers can't just walk away when it is convenient. It's a choice. A decision. And now it was my turn to choose. My parents buried their attachment to me long ago, but I cut the cord, finally, in this very moment. I was free.

I turned away from them to Charles. "I will wait for you outside. Call someone else so we can go."

"Righty-o. In fact, Kovach is probably dying for something else to prove. He can watch them."

Charles's eyes met mine, and he lightened my mood.

I turned back to the people who left me for a life of service. Their daughter, the ultimate sacrifice, a younger version of myself, gifted to them at birth. And they walked away.

I beamed, as I clenched my fists, steeling my nerves, "Thank you. You taught me so much in your absence that I'm exactly who I am supposed to be. See you next lifetime."

I meant every word.

Chapter Twenty-Two

I HAD BEEN GRANITE INSIDE THE PRISON WALLS, BUT OUT HERE with him, I cried softly into his shirt. I had just faced the people who kept my life in darkness for so long. And I was out here, in the light. And Charles brought me back.

"Come on, honey." Charles said, "Do you want to talk about it, Sofia?"

"You know I do, but for now let's just enjoy the journey home."

I'd closed a circle, learned my lesson for this lifetime. I'd returned to a friendship that had supported me for so many years. I made up a lot of karma points by visiting Joelle in the hospital. Seeing her was a catalyst, and I was ready to leave the sanctity of the camp. This period of my life had been great while it lasted, but bad things could and would happen anywhere. A small boy could be riding a bicycle, the wind blowing through his blond hair, and a landmine could take away everything in the blink of an eye.

For now, I wanted to be with Charles when bad things happened. It was all we could hope for in this life, to be with someone we trusted.

Before long, we were back in our refurbished villa in Buenos Aires, all the construction complete, and no hint of smoke or fire remained. Charles had commissioned an experienced contractor and artist from Valparaiso, his best friend, Sergio. Ms. Mendoza's lot was part of our land as well. She left it to a local charity that preferred our cash over the land. We stripped it all away to build a greenhouse in her honor. The foundation of the house remained, and Charles convinced me that the greenhouse would be sustainable for much longer.

Together we amassed over a couple million dollars, and, with Charles investing part of it, our fortune was growing by the day. I didn't care as much about having money now as I did about having peace. I reopened Ms. Mendoza's dance studio in the city. I taught cumbia, salsa, and merengue. I hired a tango instructor from one of the best studios in the city.

The man was aging gracefully but he could still dance better at sixty-five than most thirty-year-old hipsters. Charles supported the idea of the studio and the endorphins I got every day for doing something I loved. I only worked during the weekdays. Many of Ms. Mendoza's older friends used the studio gratis on the weekends. I hired Alma De La Vacos to be my assistant manager. I paid her twice what she made in the military, and I had never seen such a desperately happy young woman. I even got her moving her hips while standing at the front desk and signing people up for lessons. She had a strength I wished I had at her age, the strength to value myself above the mission. After I handed her a stack of the well-worn books I coveted, we regularly discussed our way forward. Both of us, a work in progress.

Sofia Paltrini still had a heart even after so much death.

One night, at home, Charles got up from the couch and bent over to kiss me. He was still with the agency, and I decided that it didn't matter to me. We each had to decide what was best for our short lives.

"Do you want anything from the kitchen?" he asked.

"White wine." He was making me feel hot and bothered by walking around half naked.

We were a team, and something was right about staying together. I chose this.

Charles came back with glasses of chilled Pinot Grigio.

He sat down beside me and handed me my glass.

"Let's toast!"

"To what?"

His answer was irrelevant, because I'd created my own environment—we could celebrate all the choices in our lifetimes. I was determined to keep up the good work. To find the alchemy in my story and turn it into gold.

He seemed to hesitate before lifting his glass, "To life...after so much death."

"Cin, cin."

Epilogue

Joelle Catanese

"I THOUGHT YOU WERE SOME MILITARY CHICK WHO DOESN'T CARE about the finer things in life," Gianni said, as we stopped in front of an extremely expensive but stylish boutique in Taormina, Sicilia.

"You know I am much more than a uniform, so don't start pinching pennies now," I said.

Gianni was playing the role of dutiful head of household and joking about all the money we were spending, but honestly, he enjoyed seeing me spend half our travel budget on Italian designers. The other half was spent on pistachio gelato. He gave me his approval to buy the many outfits I couldn't wear in public anywhere but here and maybe Miami. He didn't look like a slob either. We were hot honeymooners, and while I may be a small-town Midwesterner at heart, I pretended to know what style looked like. I loved our being together for so much uninterrupted time, no jobs, and no responsibilities, just us. It reminded me of the good parts of Miami, before his betrayal. It made me realize we made the right decision staying together.

"Andiamo. I want to see you in that," Gianni said. He pulled me into Calzedonia, a chain store that sold sexy silk stockings.

"Of course, you do."

That night, Gianni made love to me until dawn. It had been seven months since Kosovo, and we were wild with the romance of getting out of town. I woke up and decided to call home when I was sure they would be getting ready for bed. The seven-hour time difference isolated us further, and we were happy to enjoy our time. When I pulled out my list of numbers, I hesitated before calling my family. I had a very good friend who I could call instead. I had to see if it was possible. I dialed the long code of international numbers. It rang.

"Joey!"

"It's me, battle buddy," I said. "I was checking to see it you were telling me the truth. Can I really just dial this code and speak to you whenever I want?"

She laughed into the phone, a Latin beat playing in the background.

"Of course you can, that's why I got this phone; it's especially for you," she said.

"Where are you at now?" I asked. "I hear music?"

"My dance studio. I am teaching cumbia. You believe this is what I do all day?"

"I hope, I really hope, it's what you do all day."

"Seriously, I am out of the game," she said. "Unless someone makes an attempt on your life."

"That's not going to happen," I said, thinking about Kosovo and the car crash that almost killed me.

"I am telling you, you are safe," she said. "I would bet my life on it. You know I will always stand by you. Enough of the hard stuff, how are you?"

"The best ever!"

"Oh, I bet. You were always the optimist."

I heard a man's voice in the background.

"Who are you talking to?"

"Charles, you better stop eavesdropping or there won't be any mystery to me left," she yelled.

She came back to the phone.

"Sorry about that," she said. "It looks like someone stopped by to surprise me at work. This is a new relationship for us, and we're not used to boundaries like girl talk and all."

"That sounds like fun. All I care about is, are you happy, battle buddy?"

"Yes, I am, finally," she said. "You were right about getting out when you did."

"You were also right," I said, suddenly sentimental. "I needed to do a few things before I could live on that farm I bought. Iraq wasn't the end of the world. I had to see for myself. I had to learn to not be a coward."

"I don't want to hear you call yourself a coward, girl. Some grown men don't have balls as big as we do. Listen, we were both right," she said. "You were the brave one staying home. You chose what was right for you."

"Sometimes I asked myself why I volunteered for that last deployment with you, and then let you go on all the hard missions without me," I said, my chest collapsing as I considered the weight of that selfish act. "I was supposed to be there for you, watching your back."

"Joelle, I wouldn't have let you go with me even if you tried," she said. "I inherited a legacy from my family that ensured I would try to do dangerous shit. It doesn't matter that now I know they wanted something different for me."

I heard her take a deep breath, contemplating. I missed these talks.

"You have to think about it differently," she said. "Think

about it the way I think about you. Even though you were scared, you still signed up, you still hauled your ass over to the sandbox and stood behind your rifle waiting for someone to fuck with you. You were lucky. You had me. They didn't fuck with you. If it came down to it, you would have pulled the trigger, but you were so smart that you didn't have to."

"Oh, I'm smart now because I'm scared. Good to know."

"If I say you're smart, then you are. It's about being scared and still doing the job, while you're pissing yourself," she said. "It's what makes us human. Yes, soldiers, yes, women, always squared away bitches. You should be proud of yourself, Jo."

I laughed and wiped the tears from my eyes. Her wise words and familiar attitude overwhelmed me. It was hard won.

"That's right, Chapastick. Get it right, get it tight," I said, and laughed. "I miss our 'Cher in the Shower' moments, but mostly I miss running next to you on a treadmill. Gianni doesn't even let me play the one-upping game like we used to. He calls it a hamster wheel. I guess I can't run at a nine point zero anymore. On another note, when do we get to have an official visit? I want to see that studio of yours."

"I'll give you a hint, I'm still in the Americas."

"That could be anywhere," I said. "That's like the hot bed of all espionage activity."

"With that, I'll get back to work."

A long pause hung in the thick air.

"Love you."

"Love you, too. Watch your six."

"I always do."

Acknowledgments

IN MY JOURNEY, A FEW PEOPLE CARRIED ME THROUGH AS A PUB-lished author. My significant other, Tony, who never let me give up. He is my first editor and persistence coach. My grandma, Betty, the artist who gave me inspiration into how real life works and taught me how to turn it into beautiful things. This took a talented team. My editor, Latoya C. Smith with LCS Literary, who gave me a first round of courageous editing. For the entire Circuit Breaker Books team who brought my vision to life and made it a worthy read. For the Mindbuck Media team who encouraged me to get the good word out about female veteran fiction. For Deborah Jayne (Paper Jayne) for making the impossible happen. For the countless veterans who poured their heart out to me and cried happy tears for the gift of life after we were beyond sacrifice. Thank you!

Share Your Opinion

Did you enjoy *Beyond Sacrifice*? Then please consider leaving a review on Goodreads, your personal blog, or wherever readers can be found. At Circuit Breaker Books, we value your opinion and appreciate when you share our books with others.

Go to circuitbreakerbooks.com for news and giveaways.

Alicia Dill is an Army veteran, journalist, public speaker, and award-winning author. Originally from Missouri, she joined the Iowa Army National Guard at the age of seventeen. She received a degree in journalism and international studies at the University of Iowa, and has a masters from the University of Dubuque. Her first book, *Squared Away*, was a 2020 International Next Generation Indie Book Award winner and a finalist for the National Indie Excellence Award.

CPSIA information can be obtained
at www.ICGtesting.com
Printed in the USA
FSHW010159131021
83350FS